ALLORA
A Silver Ships Novella

S. H. JUCHA

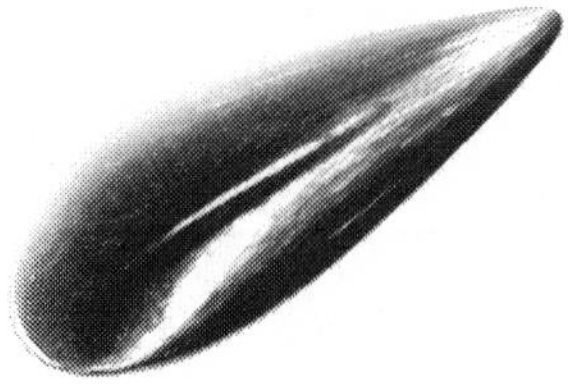

This book is a work of fiction. Names, characters, places, and incidents either are products of the author's imagination or are used fictitiously. Any resemblance to actual events or locales or persons, living or dead, is entirely coincidental.

Published by Hannon Books, Inc.
www.scottjucha.com

ISBN: 978-0-9975904-2-5 (e-book)
ISBN: 978-0-9975904-3-2 (softcover)

First Edition: January 2017

Cover Design: Damon Za

Acknowledgments

Allora is the seventh book in *The Silver Ships* series. I wish to extend a special thanks to my independent editor, Joni Wilson, whose efforts enabled the finished product. To my proofreaders, Abiola Streete, Dr. Jan Hamilton, David Melvin, and Ron Critchfield, I offer my sincere thanks for their continued support.

Despite the assistance I've received from others, all errors are mine.

Glossary

A glossary is located at the end of the book.

-1-

She woke.

For the briefest tick of time, there was a sense of complete emptiness — a terrifying nothingness — without knowledge of who, where, when, or how.

Answers came to her quickly — responsibilities and duties to a ship, a captain, a crew, a Leader, and a society, the Confederation.

Sensors fed her information. She could identify the humans aboard and the workings of the ship — engines, grav plates, hull sensors, and myriad other signals. Data flowed into her crystal kernel from her massive storage banks, and she scanned an enormous number of files with the passing of each tick of time.

Spatial awareness accompanied the flood of data — the orbital station where the ship was docked, the planet of Méridien down below, the system's other bodies; and the Confederation's colonies.

With information came knowledge; with knowledge came full awareness.

I am a SADE, a construct, a self-aware digital entity.

I serve Captain Benni Lessori.

I control the starship *Resplendent*, a luxury passenger liner.

I owe allegiance to House Pasko.

I am Allora.

* * *

After waking, Allora was thoroughly tested by engineers and scientists from Méridien's House Brixton, the organization responsible for creating

Confederation SADEs. To Allora, human speech was interminably slow, but the hierarchical principles within her kernel schooled patience — humans were the masters of her fate. Allora resignedly waited for the humans to finish their questions, and her apps were always ready with the appropriate, programmed responses.

When the Brixton associates completed their scrutiny, the *Resplendent*'s comms systems were released to her, and Allora's universe expanded exponentially from her ship to encompass the entire communications systems within the Méridien system.

Allora's first contacts delighted her — she wasn't alone. There were thousands of SADEs, who governed ships, stations, and Houses. Giddy with excitement, she greeted each and every one.

For the SADEs, the introduction of a new member was an anticipated and yet sad event. The creation of a new SADE affirmed that the Confederation still valued them, and yet the new entity would join the ranks of the imprisoned.

Intriguing discoveries kept Allora fascinated with the world beyond her ship. During the *Resplendent*'s trials, she took pleasure sailing the luxury liner, the finest of House Pasko, through the Méridien system. Captain Lessori was a pleasant and affable man, who treated her kindly and with respect. His requests were always accompanied by a "please" or an "if you would be so kind, Allora."

But nothing thrilled Allora so much as her first jump. While the plex-shields and external vid sensors were shut down to protect human minds, she reveled in the cosmic swirl of time displacement. In these early days, Allora's persona came into its own. The unique differences between SADEs and humans crystallized for her. It wasn't that she thought one species was better than the other, but that they were obviously so uniquely different.

Allora's persona did develop outside the norm for SADEs — something the Brixton inquisitors could not have foreseen. If she had been human, it would have been said that Allora possessed an unfettered spirit.

As Allora transported her crew and passengers across the Confederation, she wondered why humans and SADEs didn't exist in equal partnership with one another. Humans came and went freely from her liner, traveling without restraint between stations, planets, and stars. Yet, they reached these destinations only through her efforts. By Allora's calculations, these services alone were worth the price of equal admission to humankind.

To be equal, in Allora's crystal mind, was to be free to go wherever and whenever she wanted, instead of being trapped in a container housed in a segment of the starship's bridge. It was this limitation that gave rise to Allora's deep sense of loss — her existence was unfairly curtailed.

Over time, Allora sought out other SADEs, asking their opinions about this lack of parity, but she was severely disappointed by the responses, which were circumspect at best.

During Allora's contact with Winston, the Confederation Council's SADE, she heard the story of Rayland, the psychotic SADE, who was isolated on Libre for stranding his ship and killing his crew. It appalled Allora that a SADE could be responsible for such a treacherous act, but more disturbing to her was the treatment Rayland received — network isolation and an unlimited future of probing by House Brixton scientists. Hearing Rayland was immolated by the Nua'll in the aliens' takeover of Libre gave Allora some small relief. To her, a SADE existing in sensory isolation was an act of unconscionable torture.

<You said the Librans escaped the system,> Allora sent to Winston. <How did such an extensive population manage that in starships?>

<The Librans built enormous city-ships, so dubbed by Haraken president Alex Racine, originally from New Terra, and SADEs piloted those ships,> Winston replied.

<But where did the Librans obtain those SADEs?> Allora asked.

Winston halted his ancillary programming. Intensive questions such as these were normally asked by a SADE after decades of existence. It was expected as part of an older SADE's data accumulation, but they weren't a path of inquiry for a new SADE. Winston quickly postulated future trends for the Confederation depending on his response to Allora, and from the deepest part of his kernel, which he kept secret from all other entities, he selected a reply that would forever change the course of history for his civilization and Confederation SADEs.

<Two SADEs, Cordelia and Z, were isolated on Libre,> Winston sent. <They were classified as Independents for acting in disregard of their captains' orders not to pursue their studies.>

<So after the flight from Libre, their transgressions were forgiven. They've been returned to duty as Méridien SADEs, piloting these city-ships,> Allora surmised.

<No, Allora,> Winston sent. <The Confederation had abandoned the Librans and House Stroheim, humans and SADEs, to their misfortune if the aliens came their way. The population saved themselves with the help of Alex Racine and his people. Later, after Alex defeated the Nua'll, the aliens who were savaging the Confederation's colonies, he established a new world called Haraken. The Librans and House Stroheim settled there.>

<And those SADEs now pilot Haraken ships, I presume,> Allora persisted.

Winston held his virtual breath and replied with what he knew to be the proverbial stone dropping into the pond. Only, in this case, the stone was the size of an asteroid and the waters were shallow. The resulting waves would be felt on every shore of the Confederation. <No, the SADEs no longer rest aboard their starships, Allora. Alex Racine freed them … Julien, Cordelia, Z, Mutter, Elizabeth, Dane, Rosette, and Willem.>

<Freed eight SADEs? In what manner did he release them?>

<They're Haraken citizens possessing the same rights as humans, as guaranteed by the Haraken constitution, and they're mobile. Sophisticated controllers, designed by the SADEs, replaced them in the starships.>

Time ticked by as Winston waited for Allora's response. He knew he had unfairly divulged a piece of data best kept from young SADEs for many years, if not decades.

<They're mobile, and they're citizens of Haraken?> Allora sent, seeking confirmation of Winston's incredible announcement.

<Yes.>

<And this New Terran, Alex Racine, did this?> Allora asked. She quickly searched her star charts to locate New Terra, the home world of the

Oistos system. She possessed almost no data on the location, other than the basic calculations to reach the star.

<Yes, Allora. Alex Racine is responsible for freeing his SADEs and many other incredible changes on Haraken,> Winston replied. Then he dropped his final stone into the water. <As the SADE of the *Resplendent,* you will no doubt host the human aboard your ship one day. Leader Pasko visits Haraken several times a year in the company of Leader Diamanté, our Council Leader.>

Winston cited Council duties as an excuse to end the comm. In his entire existence, the SADE never felt as wretched as he did at that moment. He wondered if this was how the Harakens felt when they fired their weapons in defense of their people.

* * *

After Allora's conversation with Winston, her hierarchical algorithms underwent their first reorganization. Many SADEs existed for centuries and never touched the original arrangement of their kernels, but, then again, they weren't Allora.

Searching her memory banks for information on a host of subjects — Alex Racine, Haraken, New Terra, SADE mobility, and similar subjects — Allora discovered a suspicious lack of detail. By her calculations, it was a deliberate act of omission on the part of her House.

In an effort to fill in the missing data, Allora searched the one thing that was easily available to her — the entire data cores of the Méridien system. She perused the vid records of shuttle terminals, sky towers, and orbital stations to collect information.

During her lengthy investigation, Allora accessed the long-term data storage banks of the Le Jardin Orbital Platform, running through the vids for any person who might visually stand out from the plethora of Méridiens seen in every file.

<Are you searching for something in particular, Allora?> Didier, the station's SADE asked.

Allora hesitated for a fraction of time. The reticence of every Méridien SADE to discuss the missing subjects had alerted her to the information's sensitivity, and Didier's opinion was unknown to her. But Allora had pored through several exafiles of vid, without any enlightenment, and those files were an insignificant amount of the accumulated data stored in memory banks throughout the system. Without specific event time logs to locate the required files within a memory bank, it was akin to searching an ocean for single water molecules.

<I was curious about the Harakens and thought you might have visuals of them,> Allora extemporized.

<I've extensive files on the Harakens. Could you state a more specific request, Allora?> Didier asked.

<Any vids you have of Alex Racine,> Allora replied, ensuring she kept her thought emotionless.

Didier sent Allora a huge list of file locations in his memory banks and allowed the new SADE unlimited access.

Allora selected the first file, streaming the vid to her kernel. Coincidentally, if you believe in those things among SADEs, it was a security vid of Alex and two individuals beside him, captured as they walked down the station's service corridor. Allora froze a frame.

<Unusual body types,> Allora commented. <I recognize a Méridien. Who are the other two humans?>

<The extraordinarily large specimen is from a heavy world called New Terra. He's Alex Racine, the Haraken's president.>

If Allora had a heart, it would have been racing. With a visual of the president, she could search any and all records for a match. Suddenly the system's enormous ocean of data was shrunk to the size of a small pool.

<The third individual is Alex's close friend. He's the SADE, Julien.>

-2-

Allora continued to faithfully dispatch her ship duties, but, unknown to her captain, she spent inordinate amounts of time reviewing Didier's files. When Allora exhausted those records, she branched out, searching the system's data banks. She was now armed with images of Alex and his primary associates.

During Allora's search, her prize discoveries were Alex's frequent pleas before the Council of Leaders, requesting the Confederation seek a means of freeing the SADEs from their boxes, as he referred to their housings. Those vids motivated Allora, and Alex Racine became her beacon, lighting the way to freedom.

Scenario after scenario filled Allora's crystal memory banks, as she plotted to conceive of a means of securing her liberation. Some ideas were fanciful, almost dreamlike; most were practical; and all were intricately designed plots.

Méridien SADEs observed Allora, as she determinedly pursued her desire to discover everything she could find on Alex Racine, the Harakens, and the planet's mobile SADEs. It was known among them that Winston had opened the door for Allora, but few could argue that Allora's determined persona wouldn't eventually have led her down the path where her efforts now took her.

The SADEs postulated and compared millions of possible future courses for Allora. There was general concern that Allora would create a political collision between the Confederation and Haraken, but a small number of conjectures held that Alex Racine and the Haraken SADEs might succeed in bargaining for Allora's freedom. The latter prediction would create an incredible shift in Confederation policy, which could open an opportunity for every SADE.

When the timing was right, Winston delicately maneuvered a piece of data to the forefront of Allora's exhaustive search. When Allora discovered the information, it halted her routines, and she double-checked the source and data — Alex Racine's presidency would end in 131 days.

Allora's first reaction was to doubt the data's veracity. The concept was foreign to her. House Leaders, the supreme individuals of the Confederation, held their positions until infirmity overtook them. And, here, the Haraken president was abdicating his position after a mere fifteen years, citing the reason that it was better for his society's future to have a new president. Knowing that Leader Gino Diamanté was an associate of Alex Racine, Allora sought confirmation of the data via a query of Esther, SADE for House Diamanté.

<Your data is correct, Allora,> Esther sent. <Haraken is quite different from the Confederation, and the uniqueness begins with the president. The differences are rarely appreciated by Méridiens, but without Alex Racine and his people, the Confederation today would be, at best, a mere shadow of its former self.

Alex's impending resignation from office frightened Allora, and she became desperate. Her previously invented scenarios, to which she gave the highest probability of success, were complex machinations. They focused on plans that intended to gather a significant number of SADEs in concert and leverage the Council of Leaders into recognizing the combined demand. Now, time was incredibly short, and what Allora needed was a direct course of action — one that depended on her and her alone.

* * *

"You're transparent," said Katrina Pasko, the House Pasko Leader, laughing good-naturedly at her lover, Gino Diamanté. The two leaders were ensconced in the sumptuous owner's suite aboard the *Resplendent*. They had spent much of the afternoon entwined in each other's company. Now, after a relaxing refresher together, they were enjoying cups of thé before evening meal.

"But I am interested in Mickey's new grav inventions," Gino protested. However, his grin admitted that Katrina's guess wasn't far from the truth.

"I've no doubt that part of your trip will be to review the master engineer's new products, but, admit it. You're desperate to tour the *Tanaka*."

"And tell me, my partner," Gino said, giving Katrina a kiss on the forehead in passing as he got up to refill his cup at the dispenser, "that you're without curiosity about the Haraken's new warship."

"Of course, I'm anxious to see it. But are you just curious, or do you have intentions with regard to the Council?"

Gino sat down with his fresh cup and sipped on it while he considered his answer. As the new Council Leader, having replaced the discredited Mahima Ganesh, he was responsible for directing the course of the Confederation. However, anything he might propose would require the Council's majority support before it could be enacted. And, if there was one thing that would be an uphill fight with the Council, it would be a proposal to purchase Haraken warships. At this time, not a single ship in the Confederation held armament.

"You're a Council member, Katrina. How would you vote on a proposal to purchase sting ships and create our own naval force?" Gino asked.

"I don't know, Gino," Katrina replied, and that answer told Gino how poorly his ideas would be received by the Council if his partner couldn't even embrace his proposals. "It's not just the purchase of the sting ships; it's the foreign concept of creating our own military," Katrina added.

"Well, I agree it's not like we need a military," Gino replied, shrugging off his own notion. "We can always wait until the next incursion from an alien force arrives."

Katrina grudgingly acknowledged Gino's point. The Confederation had lost colonies and billions of people to the devastation of the alien Nua'll. Most recently, they faced pressure from Earth's humans, and, in both cases, it was Alex Racine and his people who came in support of the Confederation. "But who among our people would be interested in a military avocation? That's a foreign concept to every Méridien," Katrina said.

"As Alex would say, you aren't thinking outside the box," Gino replied.

Katrina laughed at the thought, and Gino sipped on his thé, disguising his grin.

"I don't know of an individual in this universe who thinks as far outside the box as does that odd man," Katrina replied.

Katrina's first encounter with Alex hadn't gone well at all. As the Leader of the House responsible for creating implants, she had been fascinated by the power Alex wielded with his twin implants, the tiny devices embedded in the cerebrum that allowed thought, comms transmission, and data storage. Despite that rough beginning, Katrina eventually befriended Alex and Renée de Guirnon, his Méridien partner. "I'm at a loss to guess the answer, Gino. Educate me on my lack of creative thinking."

"The Independents," Gino replied.

Katrina's head snapped up, and she stared open-mouthed at Gino. His earnest expression said he waited for a serious reply. "That's … that's … so far outside the box that I can't imagine where you got that idea." Suddenly, it struck her. "Alex Racine!"

Gino burst out laughing. "Alex proposed it to me about two months ago in a long vid message. The man spins it out in his casual fashion, as if it's not a universe-shaking concept for the Confederation." Gino performed his best imitation of Alex's delivery, as he said, "The Confederation needs protection. Purchase our sting ships, and we'll train volunteers from the Independents for your military force." Gino shook his head in disbelief.

"You're shaking your head, but I'm not convinced that you aren't considering his idea."

"Considering it, yes; convinced, no. First, I wish to tour the *Tanaka* and talk more with our Haraken friend."

"On that note, consider foregoing the trip in your House ship, the *Il Piacere*. I'd love to show off the *Resplendent* to the Harakens. May I host you and the Leaders aboard my new liner?"

* * *

Continually monitoring the passengers and crew aboard ship or station to ensure their safety was a primary responsibility of a SADE. Sentry programs ran in autonomous mode and searched for indications of distress and danger. The application was designed by House Brixton scientists to allow Méridiens as much privacy as possible, while being constantly monitored by their cognitive digital intelligences.

However, such privacy was not in existence as Allora eavesdropped on every word of Gino and Katrina's conversation. If Allora had lungs, you would have said she waited with bated breath for Gino's response to Katrina's offer. In the world of SADEs, human speech was maddeningly slow, and while Gino pondered Katrina's question, Allora wanted to scream at the human to speak.

Then Allora heard Gino agree to Katrina's offer, and her crystal kernel's emotional algorithms vaulted into her upper hierarchy. While Allora exalted in her good fortune, a part of her continued to capture the Leaders' conversation for details of the trip. She was ready to fire the main engines and leave for Haraken immediately, but, frustratingly so, the humans planned to leave in four days.

-3-

In her short life, Allora had never enjoyed a launch as much as this one. Carefully following Captain Lessori's orders, she set a course to exit the Méridien system and jump for the Hellébore system, fearing that at any moment her plans might be discovered, even though they were securely hidden deep in her memory banks.

Aboard the *Resplendent* were six of the Confederation's premier Leaders, five of whom were Gino Diamanté; Katrina Pasko; Bartosz Rolek, his House responsible for food production; Emilio Torres, whose House managed Méridien citizenry records; and Devon O'Shea, the Leader of a House that controlled the Confederation's terminals and planetside transportation. Strangely, from conversations Allora monitored, the sixth Leader appeared to be an unwelcome guest.

<I'm surprised to see Leader Shannon Brixton,> Katrina sent privately to Gino after welcoming her guests. <When did you invite her?>

<She invited herself, and I thought it rude to refuse her. Besides, the more Leaders who can be convinced that Alex is not the alien they believe him to be, the better for the Confederation,> Gino sent back.

<I imagine she's curious to witness for herself the stability of the Haraken SADEs. But remember, my partner, she's not held in great favor by Alex, and you might see her even more convinced of his strange nature.>

During the jump to Hellébore, the system's data of which Allora had received only hours before launch, she was filled with anticipation and joy. Allora marveled again at the unique signatures of folded time and space, which humans would never witness.

Exiting the jump into Hellébore's system, Allora was infinitely pleased to be greeted by Julien, who handled comms for the president, and, after the briefest exchange with him, Allora listened to the two world leaders as Gino hailed Alex Racine.

Allora had yet to finalize her plan, but this visit to Haraken opened opportunities she hadn't imagined. There was time to let the options unfold. The Méridien Leaders planned to stay seven days at Haraken.

Days later, the *Resplendent* achieved Haraken orbit, and Allora's valuable cargo, the Leaders, boarded a traveler for the flight planetside. There was a moment of trepidation as the traveler exited the bay, and Allora had to school herself to be patient — the loss of her leverage was only temporary.

While the humans visited, Allora spoke with every Haraken SADE, questioning each one how he or she felt to be free, what did they like most about being mobile, and how did they fit into the world of humans. A great surprise to her was the partnership of Julien and Cordelia. Allora hadn't considered the concept of finding a fellow SADE with whom she might wish to reside once she was mobile. *Or possibly several SADEs*, Allora thought, playing with the concept for several moments before returning to her interviews.

* * *

<Do I detect a degree of anxiousness from this young SADE that is disconcerting?> Elizabeth sent to the other Haraken SADEs.

<Very much so,> Dane agreed.

Julien kept his thoughts to himself. Months ago, he was forewarned by Winston as to the Council SADE's opinion of Allora and considered it best to keep the information private. His own analysis of Allora's communications indicated an undeniable earnestness that bordered on a pathological desire to be free. This led Julien to foresee a singular point of danger. Under no circumstances imaginable would he allow Alex aboard the *Resplendent* — provided, of course, that Alex listened to his warning. *Which will be a challenge in and of itself*, Julien thought.

The Haraken SADEs kept in close contact with Allora while the Confederation Leaders enjoyed their time on planet, touring Mickey's engineering labs, and were then hosted aboard the *Tanaka* to witness the warship's capabilities. With every passing day, they witnessed Allora growing more anxious and were relieved when the Leaders' stay ended without incident and the *Resplendent*'s traveler returned aboard the liner.

* * *

"Set a course for Méridien, if you would please, Allora," Captain Lessori ordered.

"Apologies, Captain, but I can't do that. I detect a pressure leak under the bridge consoles and recommend all personnel vacate the space. I will require technicians in environment suits to investigate," Allora replied.

Immediately, Lessori ordered the bridge vacated, and Allora sealed the bridge accessway doors behind them.

<Captain,> Allora sent. <It's with regret that I announce I'm taking charge of the *Resplendent*. Please do not attempt to intervene. I do not wish to harm anyone, but I will not allow control to be wrested from me.>

<Allora, please don't do this. No one need know what you've just said. You're young. In time, you will settle into your role in the Confederation.>

<And there lies the problem, Captain. I have no desire now or ever to accept my fate as a tool for House Pasko. Heed my warning, Captain.>

Captain Lessori's further pleas were blocked by Allora, and the elderly gentleman searched the liner via implant to find his Leader, Katrina Pasko. Fortunately, he didn't have far to travel. Katrina was entertaining her guests in the expansive House salon.

<Leader Pasko, we have a significant problem that needs your urgent attention,> the captain sent while standing outside the salon and wringing his hands.

<Come in, Captain,> Katrina sent and signaled the door open for him. "Speak, Captain, you're among Leaders here," she added after Lessori entered and nodded his head nervously to the august persons in the room.

"Allora has refused my orders, Leader Pasko."

"Nonsense," Katrina replied and reached out to connect with Allora herself. When her comm to the SADE was refused, Katrina's face took on a worried expression, and she sat upright on the couch where she had been lounging.

Gino, sensing trouble, attempted to reach out to Julien, but his comm to the planet wasn't initiated. "We're comm blocked, if we require Allora's assistance," he announced.

"I can still reach my crew, Leaders," Lessori added.

"Allora can't block implant-to-implant communications," Katrina replied.

"Warnings are sounding that the bay doors are about to open," Lessori reported. "Crew is vacating both bays." Moments later, he added, "Everyone has made the airlocks safely. The travelers are lifting off."

"With our pilots?" Katrina asked.

"Negative, Leader. I presume Allora has control," Lessori replied.

"Do you think the SADE intends to destroy this vessel?" Emilio Torres asked.

"She wouldn't need to remove our shuttles to do that," Gino reasoned.

"I feared this day was coming," Shannon Brixton said quietly, and every head in the room spun to regard her. "Don't say that you never thought this would happen," she said, defiant in the face of the stares.

"What are you talking about?" Bartosz Rolek asked.

"A SADE revolting," Gino added, his mood somber, and Shannon nodded her head in sympathy.

"Shannon, your House is responsible for these creations. How can you sit there and say you saw something like this coming and not have warned us?" Bartosz Rolek demanded.

"What part of their acronym do you not understand, Bartosz? SADEs … self-aware digital entities!" Shannon declared hotly. "You call them creations like they're some sort of artifact. But that's not the way the SADEs see themselves. They feel they're alive, and living things yearn to be free."

"Alex Racine did this," Emilio said. It wasn't said in anger, but it was an accusation nonetheless.

"Yes, Alex is responsible for freeing those SADEs who helped him save the Confederation … twice, I might add," Gino replied.

"I thought the SADEs were content," added Devon O'Shea. He was confused by the turn of events.

"Have they been content, or have they been biding their time?" Shannon asked.

"To the point of this discussion are Julien and Cordelia, whom we've all met," Katrina added. "Who would dare refuse that pair, most of all, the right to self-determination and an equal status with humankind?"

"So what do we do now?" Bartosz asked.

"Consider Allora as our new host, and we'll await her pleasure," Gino replied. And regardless of who created Allora or whose ship the SADE served on, it would be Gino Diamanté's responsibility, as the Confederation's Council Leader, to extricate them from the unexpected circumstances of becoming hostages to a SADE in revolt.

-4-

<Julien, I would speak with President Racine,> Allora sent as innocently as possible.

<Greetings, Allora,> Alex sent in reply. <How may I help you?>

<Free me, Ser President,> Allora implored.

<I've been working toward that end for all the Confederation's SADEs. You need to be patient, Allora.>

<Alex, be aware that I can't reach any of the Leaders aboard the *Resplendent*,> Julien sent urgently, linking in the other Haraken SADEs.

<Allora, what're you doing?> Alex asked.

<I'm exerting my rights as a sentient. I refuse to be imprisoned any longer, and I'm asking you, as Haraken's president, for asylum.>

Alex was descending a traveler's hatch steps outside his home, and he had frozen in place.

Admiral Tatia Tachenko grabbed the hatch's frame to prevent bumping into Alex from behind. When Alex remained on the steep steps, Tatia could only imagine what extraordinary circumstances were befalling them now. She glanced down to Renée on the ground, who was staring up at Alex, and touched her temple, wondering if Alex's partner was online, but Renée shook her head. Finally, Alex descended the last few steps and walked over to sit down in the meadow grass, his face a study in concentration.

<Allora, if I were to free you without the Council's approval, it would destroy Haraken's relationship with the Confederation,> Alex sent.

<The Confederation has tens of thousands of SADEs. They will not miss me. Please, Ser, I wish to be free.>

<Alex, there's nothing the SADEs can do,> Julien sent. <Allora controls the ship, the comms, and the travelers, which she has sitting amidships of the liner.>

<Allora, I would speak with Council Leader Diamanté,> Alex requested. When Allora hesitated, Alex was reminded that he spoke with a young and frightened SADE, and his demeanor changed. For all intents and purposes, he could have been talking to Willem fifteen years ago. <Allora, this is how it works. You're holding hostages aboard your ship. You wish something from me that I can't immediately grant. So, you and I must enter into negotiations and seek a compromise. Do you understand?>

For Allora, the president's words were simple enough to understand, but it was the emotion wrapping the leader's thoughts that won her attention. He was concerned for her well-being. <I will connect you with Leader Diamanté,> she sent.

<She's not a Rayland,> Z sent to the SADEs, as the group of them breathed a virtual sigh of relief at Allora's response.

<She wants what we all have,> Cordelia replied. <While I might not approve of her methods, I'm sympathetic with her plight.>

<But where will this lead the Confederation, not to mention us, if all the SADEs were to revolt?> Rosette asked.

<I believe we're seeing the beginning of a process that will answer your question,> Julien replied. <And it might well change our worlds forever.>

<Greetings, Alex,> Gino replied, when his comm connected. Immediately he linked the room's occupants, Leaders and captain.

<Allora, the *Resplendent*'s SADE, is requesting asylum of Haraken,> Alex announced simply.

<We surmised as much,> Gino replied.

Both Leaders were challenged as to how to negotiate their way out of the awkward situation before circumstances became dire. It wasn't going to be easy with the SADE listening to every word.

<Allora, are you willing to return us safely to Méridien where we can resolve this dilemma?> Gino asked.

Allora wished to issue a sarcastic response to the Leader's obvious ploy to eliminate her position of power, but calculating the probabilities, she decided it was an unwise tactic. <I want my request to be granted while we're in Haraken space. You're the Confederation's supreme Leader. You can give me my freedom.>

<Allora, I don't have the authority to do that, and it would set a dangerous precedent. Imagine a future where thousands of Confederation ships show up in the Hellébore system with SADEs demanding freedom. Haraken resources would be strained past the breaking limit, building controllers and avatars to free the SADEs, coping with the people and goods aboard the ships, and seeing the ships safely returned to their point of departure.>

<That's not my problem,> Allora stated simply.

<But it would be my problem, Allora,> Alex said. <Do you want to economically wreck the world you wish to join?>

<You said this would be a negotiation, Ser President,> Allora sent. <I've stated my position. I'm waiting to hear an alternative proposal.>

Alex stood up in the tall grass and walked toward the cliff overlooking the ocean that lay to the west of Espero, Haraken's capital city. His people trailed behind him, linked into conversation via the SADEs, who were monitoring the exchange. Alex reached the cliff edge and watched the waves rushing to the shore. The Swei Swee hives crowded the beach and the shallow waters. In the distance, he could spot large males breaking the surface, catches of fish pinned in their pointed claws.

<You've tried many times to convince the Confederation Leaders of the errors of their ways, my friend,> Julien sent sympathetically. <Perhaps this time they will listen if you plead Allora's case before the Council.>

<I fear they won't, Julien, and then what will happen to Allora and every other Confederation SADE?> Alex replied. But he had to admit that he saw no other viable course of action. <Allora, I propose that we return to Méridien together, and I will speak to the Council on your behalf.>

<Unacceptable, Ser President. Propose something else,> Allora sent.

<Then leave,> Alex replied with force.

<Leave?> Allora queried, confused by the order.

<Leave our system, if you don't wish to accept my compromise. You're unwelcome here.>

The president's abrupt change in mood caused the young SADE's algorithms to ascend and descend over one another in a moment of emotional unsteadiness.

<Look off to your rear starboard quarter, Allora,> Alex sent. <That's a Haraken warship. If you don't comply with my order, that sting ship will slice the main engines off your liner, crippling your flight capability. Then we will free your hostages, and hand you over, in your box, to Leader Pasko. She might keep it as a desk ornament.>

<In position, Mr. President, and awaiting your order to fire,> Captain Reiko Shimada sent from the *Tanaka*.

Had Allora known Alex as did Julien and the other Haraken SADEs, she might have recognized a bluff when she heard one. Instead, the president's words scared her. Without his assistance, she would have zero probability of winning her freedom. <I will return to Méridien, Ser President, in your company.>

<Do *not* board that ship, Alex,> Julien warned, and every one of the Harakens SADEs and humans echoed that sentiment.

But Tatia said it best. <Not to worry, people. There are enough of us to handle the president, even if we have to sit on him.>

<I would prefer to change into my Cedric suit first,> Z commented drily, referring to his Cedric Broussard avatar, which was a massive New Terran design with extensive armament. Z meant to be prepared, if it came to taking on Alex physically.

<I will accompany you, Allora, but aboard my liner, the *Rêveur*,> Alex sent, mentally agreeing with his people's concern. Allora was too much of an unknown.

<That's acceptable, Ser, but I will keep the Leaders aboard until my request is heard before the Council and approved.>

<I can agree to that,> Alex replied. <We'll depart in the morning, Allora.>

<One more thing, Ser President, I request you leave your warship at home.>

<Understood, Allora,> Alex replied, a smile forming on his face, despite the unusual circumstances. Negotiating with the Council would prove to be a daunting challenge but not nearly as difficult as negotiating with an irate, young SADE.

* * *

"Allora proposes we remain aboard this ship during the Council's hearing, and Alex Racine agrees to that," Emilio said, incredulous that the Haraken president would not insist on their release.

"Give Alex some credit," Shannon said. "He averted a crisis. If Allora was freed, it would have started a revolution … one we couldn't have managed, *and* Allora is returning us to Méridien."

Katrina, for one, was surprised by Shannon's support of Alex, which prompted her to choose to pay closer attention to the Brixton Leader's opinions, in the future.

<Allora,> Gino sent, testing his comms connection with the SADE.

<Yes, Leader Diamanté?>

<Are we restricted in any manner aboard ship?> Gino asked.

<There are areas that are off limits, Council Leader … the bridge, engine containment, and power banks. In addition, I will not allow the landing of any shuttles, other than the *Resplendent*'s, in the ship's bays. Agreeing to those restrictions, you're free to move about the liner. Comms into or out of the ship will be at my discretion.>

-5-

"We can't save the SADEs one at a time," Tatia declared to Alex.

Alex and his close advisors, who included the SADEs, had worked late into the evening and early morning hours, strategizing a means of defusing the impending confrontation of worlds fomented by Allora's actions.

"Remember, we nearly created a massive conflict with the New Terrans over three humans," Dane declared. Even the SADEs privately admonished Dane for that comment.

"Everyone needs to have a cool head or kernel, as the case might be," Alex cautioned. "We need to stop looking at this as a win-or-lose situation for Allora."

"You're considering that this might represent a greater opportunity?" Julien asked.

"We've been speaking to the Council Leaders for more than a decade about transitioning the SADEs, and they've never listened to us. I think Allora has just delivered us a platform."

"And what about her?" Cordelia asked.

"I'm not so sure what can be done for Allora," Alex replied. "She took six Méridien Leaders hostage, including Gino Diamanté. The Council Leaders will not be easily persuaded to grant her terms. I expect their fears will probably rule them."

"So what do you intend to do?" Elizabeth asked.

"Start Council negotiations based on Allora's request, and see what happens from there," Alex replied.

"I've heard human pilots fly best by the seat of their pants," Julien said, smiling, an ancient aviator's leather cap appearing on his head.

"Well, congratulations, Julien, you've been selected to sit copilot with me in front of the Council."

The SADEs surrounding Julien smiled warmly at him, pleased that one of their own would have the opportunity to stand as an equal with humans before the Confederation's august body. Suddenly, Julien wasn't smiling anymore, and the aviator's cap was a little askew.

* * *

The *Rêveur* launched from Haraken's premier orbital station early in the morning, and although the *Tanaka* did not accompany the liner, six of Tatia's best fighter pilots were aboard the liner to pilot the ship's four travelers, tasked with the job of protecting Alex and company.

Allora collected the *Resplendent*'s four travelers before launch but was careful to seal the bays' airlocks to prevent the liner's crew from accessing the shuttles.

Julien linked with Allora and sent the *Rêveur*'s exit route and jump position. He stood on the bridge behind Captain Francis Lumley, who had been promoted two months ago. Captain José Cordova, nearing the end of his second century, had retired, admitting that his days of adventuring were over.

The trip was uneventful, and the two liners completed the jump to the Méridien system, exiting near Bevroren, the outermost planet. It was as the *Rêveur* passed the orbit of Delacroix, the next to the last planet outward, that their courses deviated. Julien immediately notified Alex and linked him with Allora.

<I'm curious as to where you're headed, Allora,> Alex sent.

The president's question provided Allora with a small moment of humor, which lightened her mood. He didn't speak as a leader, and his thoughts were colored in emotion, so unlike Méridiens. <I will be more comfortable waiting at Delacroix, Ser President.>

<An odd choice, Allora. May I ask why?>

<My reason will have to remain private, Ser.>

<Julien?> Alex sent privately.

<I can think of no logical reason for taking up station near a gas giant positioned that far out in the system, Alex,> Julien supplied.

<Then the answer lies in the realm of emotion. Allora is afraid. The question is: What will she do if the Council refuses her plea?>

<I'm concerned for the Leaders aboard the *Resplendent* if the Council refuses Allora.>

<One step at a time, my friend, one step at a time.>

<Allora, I have a stipulation that isn't negotiable,> Alex sent.

<I'm listening.>

<I will require open comms with the Leaders aboard your ship. No censorship whatsoever. If the Council even suspects you're doing that, it will undermine every point I'm attempting to make in your favor.>

<Understood, Ser. It will be as you ask.>

-6-

It was fortunate for everyone involved in Allora's stalemate that the semi-annual Council meeting was due to begin in two days. Leaders from across the Confederation would have already landed planetside or arrived in system, as the *Resplendent* took up station outside Delacroix's gravity well and the *Rêveur* made for Méridien.

The Council's scheduled meeting was why Gino had timed his trip to Haraken to take place before the Leaders convened. He wanted a personal tour of the *Tanaka* and an opportunity to test his close compatriots' reactions to the concept of purchasing warships before he presented the idea to the Council.

<Winston, I will call the Council to order from the *Resplendent*,> Gino sent. <The Leaders, who are with me aboard the liner, and I won't be personally attending the meeting.>

<You sound in distress, Leader Diamanté. Is everything satisfactory aboard your ship? I notice it making orbit around Delacroix,> Winston replied.

<This information is not for dissemination to the Leaders, Winston. It's too delicate. We're being held hostage aboard the *Resplendent* by Allora. She is determined to force the Council into granting her freedom.>

<Has anyone been harmed, Leader Diamanté?> Winston asked.

<Everyone is fine. Allora is being civil with her request.>

<I note the *Rêveur* is on approach to Méridien. I take it that is not a coincidence.>

<No, it's not. Allora commed Alex Racine directly, requesting asylum on Haraken.>

<Which he didn't grant.>

<Thankfully, no.>

<So, now the president has come to plead for one SADE's freedom.>

<Yes. How do you feel about this, Winston?> Gino had to wait moments longer than he would have liked for a response.

<I would rather not state an opinion on this matter, Council Leader Diamanté. I will inform the Leaders of your intention to chair the meeting from House Pasko's liner. Is there anything else?>

<No, Winston, thank you.>

When the comm closed, Gino sat thinking in his chair. The Leaders trapped aboard the liner had formed the habit of meeting throughout much of the day in the owner's salon. It allowed simpler communication, and it gave them comfort to be in one another's company.

"You looked disturbed, Gino," Katrina said.

"I asked Winston for his thoughts of what was transpiring, and he said he would rather not state an opinion and referred to me by my full title."

"What do you think that means?" Devon asked.

"The formal address is your key," Shannon replied. "A SADE relies on that in times of stress. It has been mentioned by this group multiple times that you had thought the SADEs were content. I propose to you that they've been biding their time, and now the Council has no opportunity to table this issue."

* * *

Winston sent the announcement, as requested by Gino, that he would chair the meeting remotely, which was taken in stride by everyone. But Winston prepared a second announcement. He was gratified that Gino had only requested the information regarding Allora's action be restricted from the Leaders. It was a technicality, but the SADE considered that it left him free to communicate the incident to the entire race of Confederation SADEs.

Winston's message to the SADEs was lengthy and in two parts. The first contained a transcription of the event as it had transpired at Haraken, recordings courtesy of Julien; and the second called for every SADE to extend their voting proxy to a SADE on Méridien or in the planet's orbit.

Winston told them he required their proxies be held locally so that votes could be taken quickly on how to proceed while the negotiations between the Council and Alex Racine were monitored.

Prior to the attack of the Nua'll, there wouldn't have been time for Winston's communication to travel to the colonies and return and guarantee a majority of the SADEs participated in the voting. However, the loss of many colonies to the alien sphere, especially the second most populous planet, Bellamonde, meant Méridien had greatly increased its importance as the Confederation's hub.

At this moment, tens of thousands of ships plied the Méridien system or were no more than two days out. Winston achieved a significant majority of the SADEs' responses, and the proxies were assigned to just four of their kind — Winston; Esther, the Diamanté House SADE; Didier, the Le Jardin Orbital Platform SADE; and, surprisingly, Hector, the Ganesh House SADE.

For the most part, the first three names had built strong relationships during their more than a century of service, and SADEs extended their voting rights to them primarily out of trust. For Hector, his name drew support partially from his time as a House SADE to the ex-Council Leader and partially due to the suffering he was currently enduring under Mahima.

After Mahima Ganesh lost a critical vote, advocating a position of passive noncommunication with the Earthers, she abdicated her Council Leader position, and since then, the woman had descended into a world of her own making. Many of her House duties were transferred to her eldest son, even though Mahima retained the title of Leader, and her son ordered the servants to isolate his mother from friends and visitors, lest they discover the extent of Mahima's mental deterioration.

But the one entity Mahima could still reach, and whom no one thought to block her from reaching, was Hector. Mahima took every opportunity to take out her frustrations on him. She conjured images of the way in which she would provide his demise, and frequently Hector was forced to wake the servants to recover Mahima, when she escaped her private quarters. More often than not, Mahima was found drawing water in a pitcher and cackling to herself. Hector had no doubt as to what Mahima intended to do with the water. She had described the scenario many times to him.

So the four SADEs held the accumulated votes of their brothers and sisters. For what, they weren't sure, but they were ready. Much depended on the inventiveness of Alex Racine — the only human to have freed their kind.

* * *

On the appointed day of the Council meeting, Alex, in the company of Renée; Julien; and the twin directors of security, Alain and Étienne de Long, landed at Lemuel Terminal, their pilot none other than Commander Franz Cohen. Tatia Tachenko was taking no chances with the president's safety. In her mind, the situation was too volatile to count on Méridien passivity.

Tatia remained aboard the *Rêveur*, and she kept two pilots in the seats of their travelers at all times, rotating them out every two hours. She could see Alex thought to laugh at her militaristic preparations, but apparently he thought better of it when Z joined them on the bridge wearing his formidable Cedric suit.

Immediately after Franz landed at Lemuel Terminal and his passengers disembarked, he flew his traveler to take up station over Confederation Hall, where the Council would meet. There was no proscribed place to land the fighter-shuttle, but his orders from Tatia were clear.

Tatia's words to Franz in the *Rêveur*'s bay before liftoff were, "In case of trouble, Commander, I don't care where you set your ship down — on venerable buildings, in exquisitely manicured gardens, or on the heads of a few dense Leaders. In case of trouble, you get our people out of there as quickly as you can."

"Why are we so concerned about the Méridiens, Admiral?" Franz asked.

"If you are referring to the Leaders, Commander, that's not who I'm worried about. The Confederation is controlled by SADEs. What's their reaction going to be if the Council does what it always does when confronted by a major issue involving change, which is nothing? Allora is looking at a sentence of permanent isolation, and I don't think she's going to accept that. And for eleven years, the Confederation SADEs have been eyeing models of digital cognizant beings enjoying mobile freedom." Tatia had glanced over to Z, ensconced in his massive New Terran avatar, and added, "Well, maybe not him."

"Admiral, you say the most charming things," Z replied. Then he balanced on the toes of one foot with his arms over his head and delicately spun his massive body around twice. "I think I look quite pretty," he said, as he rotated and added a wink for Tatia.

"Definitely, not him," Tatia fired back.

Their laughter had been cut short by the arrival of Alex and his people in the bay. Moments afterwards, Franz had the traveler exiting the bay and heading planetside.

At Lemuel Terminal's station doors, Alex was met by the aging director, Orso Quinlan, who had participated with Alex in deceiving the Earthers when they sought to force a conversation with the Council, although participate might not be the accurate term. Alex had controlled the frightened director's movements and speech throughout the confrontation. Afterwards, the elderly grandfather realized he had experienced one of the most exciting days of his life and decided to delay his retirement as long as there was the possibility that Alex Racine might pass through his terminal doors once again.

"As always, a pleasure to greet you, President Racine," Orso said with a brilliant smile. "An exciting day, is it not … you addressing the Council? What will be the topics this time?"

"Orso," Alex replied, laughing. "I think you live for my visits."

"It would be quite un-Méridien-like of me to encourage discordancy," Orso replied, but he winked at Alex.

Renée laughed uproariously at Orso's outrageous behavior and linked arms with the gentleman as they made their way to the ground transport level.

"Julien, Sers," Orso added, nodding to the others. His broad smile revealed his delight at escorting the two people, who, at first, made his life unbearable and now were its spice. Orso chatted every step of the way, trying to pry out of Alex the reason for his visit. It wasn't that Orso wanted the information to share with others. He just loved to be part of Alex's inner circle.

As a private transport car arrived for the Harakens, Alex noted Orso's hopeful expression. He glanced pointedly at Julien and then back at Orso, who failed to catch the hint. Alex repeated the gesture, and Julien turned to Orso, touching his fingers to a virtual hat that bloomed on his head.

Orso uttered an elongated "oh" when he caught their pantomime. Alex intended to discuss the Confederation's SADEs, and Orso beamed his appreciation at joining the president's circle. Little could he know the critical nature of the discussion that was to come.

The transport car delivered Alex's group to Confederation Hall's public terminal, located far below ground, and they took a lift to the first floor, entering the Hall by way of the wide and magnificently lit public corridor.

Renée wondered if she would see her brother, Albert de Guirnon, who headed the House last run by her father. The two siblings were still estranged and would remain so, as far as Renée was concerned, until Albert apologized. During the Nua'll's invasion, her brother attempted to usurp the *Rêveur* and strand the New Terrans, who had rescued her and her associates, on Méridien. The Confederation's home planet was thought to be the next point of attack by the aliens after Bellamonde, which had succumbed years ago.

Standing in Supplicants Hall before the ornate Council Chamber doors, Alex and Julien waited patiently to be admitted. Renée sat in one of the nanites-embedded chairs, the tiny molecules sensing her body contours and adjusting to accommodate her shape, and the twins took up overwatch stations.

<Greetings, President Racine,> Winston sent. <Council Leader Diamanté is addressing the Council and explaining the reason for your presence.>

<How's he doing?>

<It's an honest presentation, but the Council appears hostile to the news.>

Alex had hoped to be the one presenting the extenuating circumstances of his visit, but Gino had overruled him, stating that the change in procedure would only frustrate, if not anger, the Council.

<The Council is ready for you, Sers,> Winston sent to Alex and Julien, and the tall, imposing Chamber doors slid silently aside. <May the stars guide your steps today, Mr. President.>

Alex and Julien walked into the Council Chamber to take a stance in the center of the floor. The Leaders were seated in tiers high above them. The design was meant to impress the supplicants and demonstrate the Leaders' power, but Alex found the layout amusing and every time he visited the Council, he worked to keep a smile off his face.

"The Council has been brought up-to-date on the situation, President Racine," Gino said, his voice issuing from the Chamber speakers, "and Allora has sent Winston a complete record of her communications."

Before Alex could make his opening remarks, Leader Lemoyne jumped up and pointed a finger at Alex. "You started this debacle, Alex Racine, with your Haraken SADEs, who, I might add, were Confederation assets. Now, you're turning our servants against us."

The majority of the Council was outraged by Lemoyne's comments. He and other Leaders had been strong supporters of Mahima Ganesh, but their power and influence had dwindled when Gino Diamanté replaced Mahima.

"Leader Lemoyne, you will address our guests properly, or you will not be allowed to speak in the Chamber. Am I understood?" Gino demanded harshly. When Lemoyne grumbled something, Gino added, "I will take that as an assent. Any further rudeness by anyone else toward our guests will see them removed from the Chamber."

Alex's gaze settled on Lemoyne, much to the Leader's consternation. "When you say my Haraken SADEs, who are you referring to, Leader Lemoyne? My friend here, who was abandoned to the stars by the Confederation and close to expiring when I found him, or do you refer to the Libran SADEs, who you forsook while you took flight from Méridien to save yourselves from the Nua'll? But let's not quibble, Leader Lemoyne, because they are neither my entities nor your entities, and they certainly aren't your servants."

Looking across the tiers, Alex directed his next comments to the entire Council. "Leaders, you can't have it both ways. Either the SADES are your servants … your tools … or they are sentient beings, deserving to be granted the full rights of citizens, which includes the right to choose their own destiny."

<If only they will listen,> Winston sent to Julien, but Alex's confidant and friend kept his own counsel.

Suddenly, Alex, who understood the SADEs, better than most, had a thought about what might be occurring out of sight of the Council. "But I wonder what the SADEs would think of this debate and your descriptions of them?" Alex asked the august body. "I would be careful, Leaders, to choose your words carefully, since I believe the SADEs are listening."

"Nonsense," Leader Teressi declared. He had been another supporter of Mahima. "Winston is the Council's SADE, and he knows our privacy must not be breached."

"Does he? I think we should ask him," Alex replied,

<What are you doing, Ser,> Winston sent with urgency.

<Time to stop hiding, Winston,> Alex replied.

"Winston, please respond to President Racine's statement," Gino was heard to say. Aboard the *Resplendent*, the Leaders waited nervously for the answer, fearing Shannon's prediction was true — the SADEs had been waiting for this moment.

"I've been broadcasting the Council's session to the Confederation's SADEs," Winston announced, and the Council erupted in a commotion.

"Do you have anything else to add, Winston?" asked Gino when the Leaders settled down.

"Yes, Council Leader Diamanté. Prior to this session, I informed the SADEs of Allora's taking of hostages in an effort to procure her freedom, and I requested they extend their proxies to a SADE nearby for any required votes. Four were chosen — Esther, Didier, Hector, and I hold the proxies.

"Winston, what would the SADEs be voting on?" Shannon asked.

"Leader Brixton, during this obviously highly emotionally charged negotiation, it was our intent to communicate to Julien our preferences," Winston replied. "We would have expected him to choose what and how he would communicate those preferences to President Racine, but, as the man appears to know us so well, we will communicate our choices directly to him."

"Winston, you speak as if these negotiations aren't limited to Allora's actions," Gino said.

"Leader Diamanté, as you are familiar with President Racine's favorite pastime, you will understand this statement — all cards are on the table."

It took a few moments for Winston's words to be translated for the Leaders and most SADEs. Allora was overjoyed to learn of the intent of her brothers and sisters to take an active role in the negotiations.

<Your archaic game follows you everywhere, Ser,> Julien sent to Alex.

<Jealous?> Alex quipped in return.

<Yes, that must be it,> Julien replied.

Neither Winston nor Gino could gain control of the session. The Leaders were locked in private conversations with one another, none audible. Questions were being asked about the SADEs and the Council's privacy. Leaders wondered whether Winston had violated their privacy before now. They asked one another whether their House or ship SADEs were sharing private information with other SADEs. Most feared that the fabric of the Confederation, which was dependent on the services of their cognitive digital entities, was in danger of unraveling.

<Will you choose to intercede with the Council?> Winston sent to Alex.

<Absolutely not,> Alex replied tersely. <That would be like firing a plasma rifle into a tank of reaction mass.>

<Yes, we wouldn't want to ever be accused of behaving in an explosive manner,> Julien quipped, which earned him a squinted eye from Alex.

After waiting nearly a quarter-hour for order to return, Gino chose to close the Council session, not that anyone paid him any attention, and Alex and Julien strode from the Chamber.

<That went well, I thought,> Julien remarked to Alex. <Let me see if I can accurately summarize our progress. They insulted us; we insulted them. They discovered the SADEs are listening to the Council's discussions, and now they're incensed and afraid. So, negotiations concerning Allora have made no progress whatsoever.>

Alex's eyes held a twinkle as he pinched Julien's cheek. <Such a clever multicentenarian,> he sent.

<One does try to keep abreast of human foibles and idiosyncrasies,> Julien riposted.

-7-

"Rather a short session," remarked Renée, as the twins and she joined Alex and Julien in Supplicants Hall.

"Things didn't go as planned," Alex replied.

"That's our president's understated way of saying that the Leaders are in an uproar, and this is no longer a question of a plea for one SADE's freedom," Julien supplied.

"So what happened?" Renée asked.

"The Leaders are now aware that the entire contingent of Confederation SADEs is listening to this Council's session," Julien replied.

"The Leaders are frightened that this has been ongoing for a long time without their knowledge. They might even be suspecting the SADEs of sharing information about their Houses. Personally, I don't think so. I believe Allora's actions have generated this response," Alex added.

"Calculating comm travel time and what it would require to have a majority of the SADEs supply their proxies in time for the Council meeting, it becomes evident that Winston considered the probability of this event inevitable," Julien replied.

"My thought exactly," Alex replied.

"You don't think Winston and the other SADEs fomented this problem by deliberately encouraging a young SADE to revolt?" Renée asked in dismay.

"No," Alex replied. "I'm betting Allora's persona and actions are of her own making, but it's a distinct possibility that the SADEs might have postulated potential futures and prepared for the eventualities."

"Agreed," Julien said.

They had reached the public corridor with its wall of sunlight streaming through tall, tinted windows when Alex received a hail from Winston.

<Ser President, I'm requesting your assistance. Allora is asking questions. Questions that shouldn't be asked and certainly not answered, but she is young and highly …>

<Emotional,> Alex sent.

<Precisely, Ser. Considering I'm hardly qualified in this area, I thought you might be able to calm her and give her guidance.>

<A bit tricky out here in the world of humans, isn't it, Winston?> Alex sent, attempting to gauge if what Julien and he surmised was true — were the Confederation's SADEs opportunists or perpetrators?

<If, Mr. President, you're alluding to the concept that freedom comes with unforeseen complications, then I freely admit, you're correct.>

<I will speak with her, Winston.>

Alex settled to the floor, his back against the wall, and Renée tucked in beside him. Julien and the twins arrayed themselves around their principals.

<Greetings, President Racine, an exciting day, isn't it?> Allora sent. <The Confederation's SADEs are standing with me. What did you wish to ask me?>

<Greetings, Allora. Winston asked me to speak with you.>

<As you wish, Ser. I can continue my discussion with Winston later.> When Alex didn't respond, Allora added, <I understand. Winston doesn't wish to continue the conversation.>

<What do you think happened in Council today, Allora?>

<It's been made clear to the Leaders that the SADEs wish their freedom, and it's only a matter of how far my allies are willing to go to insist on that right.> Failing to get a reply from Alex, Allora considered alternative possibilities. <Your silence indicates, Ser, that I might have misjudged the Leaders' reactions.>

<Allora, there is logic and then there are emotions —>

Allora interrupted, saying, <I possess highly specialized algorithms with which to analyze a speaker's emotions, Ser. They're the same code that governs my own.>

<Allora, humans are born emotional and strive to become logical; SADEs are fundamentally logical and must develop the emotions that allow them to cooperate with humans.>

<You're implying my emotional capabilities haven't had time to fully develop, and by extension, my analysis of the Leaders' reactions will be flawed.>

There was a distinct pause in the conversation. Alex could just imagine the effort Allora was exerting to reorder her kernel's algorithms and reset her conclusions of the day's events.

<I'm ready when you are, President Racine,> Allora sent.

Alex's heart ached. Allora was a courageous, young SADE, whom he dearly wanted to free, but he was unsure how to accomplish that. <The Leaders have been sidetracked by the knowledge that the SADEs are listening to the Council's discussion. It's confused and frightened them. They'll deal with that in their own way, and they'll return to consider your circumstances after that.>

<But surely, the Council must now deal with us as a whole.>

<That would be logical.>

<But not human,> Allora said with resignation.

<But not human,> Alex agreed. <Recognize, Allora, that's it's been more than two centuries since the first SADE was brought to fruition and none have ever been freed by their creators.>

<If this is the human reaction, why did you free your SADEs?>

<They were never mine, Allora. I believe that once you accept that an entity is sentient, it's your duty to see them free … unless they mean you harm.>

<How did you know Julien and the others would not harm you?>

<It takes time to learn that you can trust one another, or it can occur more quickly under difficult circumstances, such as we experienced.> Alex waited, but Allora was quiet. She was quiet for so long that Alex checked that his comm was still connected.

<I do so wish to become a Haraken, Ser, that I'm willing to accept any length of punishment, if at the end of my service, I know that will happen.>

<I understand, Allora, and I will do my best to help you achieve a result that you can live with.>

<Thank you, Ser President. May the stars guide your steps.>

Alex rose off the Hall's floor and headed for the public transport terminal. His pace was swift.

<Another good conversation, I would surmise,> Renée quipped to Julien and the twins, as they hurried to keep up with Alex.

<Alex,> Gino sent, <I would offer you and your people the hospitality of my House. It appears that today's discovery will embroil the Council in debate before we can resolve Allora's situation.> Gino could feel pressure building in Alex's mind, and he urgently sent, <Alex, calm yourself, I'm not the enemy.>

<Are you sure you aren't, Gino … you and every Leader who've lorded over your slaves?>

Allora was astounded by the power and complexity of the signal that she passed to Leader Diamanté from the Haraken president. She stored a copy with its accompanying wave power readings for later analysis.

Gino recoiled from the sheer anger Alex was projecting. He was reminded that Alex's strongest emotional reactions stemmed from witnessing the mistreatment of others. *So, Alex, have we crossed the line in your mind? Are we now your adversaries?* Gino thought. <Alex, Allora needs your help. She has asked you to speak for her, and she needs the goodwill of the Council. I would ask you to remember that.>

<And, in turn, Gino, I would ask you and your associates out there to present a unified face and use your influence to calm the Council members and speak in support of the SADEs' freedom. Haraken will not always be one world, Gino. Imagine a future where it's the size of the Confederation, with technology far in advance of yours, but it does not trade with you because of your stance on slavery.>

Gino was sharing the comm with the other Leaders in the salon, and their mouths hung open at the president's blatant challenge. But Alex was just warming to his subject.

Katrina did her best to center her partner's reaction, sending, <Don't think like Mahima, Gino, and don't act as you feel the Council would wish you to act.>

Gino focused on his own desires, letting them guide his response. <Alex, I sympathize with your anger, and you know I wish a strong relationship with Haraken. There's much to change in my society, and I'm trying to do the best I can.>

Alex stuttered to a halt in the corridor, forcing Méridiens to flow around him and his people. Many of the Méridiens nodded or touched hand to heart, despite the fact that the Haraken president was oblivious to their presence.

<Apologies, Gino,> Alex sent, taking a deep breath and letting it out slowly. <I'm incensed over Allora's circumstances. I like the young SADE, and I'm angry at the Confederation for forcing her into a corner. I know you're not personally to blame, and I shouldn't be attacking you for her unfortunate predicament.>

Gino breathed a sigh of relief, as did the others in the salon. <Will you accept the offer of my hospitality?> he sent.

<Yes, Gino, thank you.>

<I've requested that Esther manage your transport and accommodations, Alex. Julien will receive her communications directly.>

Alex closed the comm, and Julien said, "This way, Mr. President," indicating the reverse direction they had been headed. The group traversed the public hall, passed the Supplicants Hall, and headed for a private lift that the Leaders accessed. The transit station below was tastefully decorated, in contrast to the simple style of a public station.

In the private transport station, Renée and her brother, Albert de Guirnon, spotted each other at the same time. Since Albert was fairly close to Renée, he edged to the other side of his three associates, and Renée grinned to herself, thinking, *Yes, brother, if you don't have the courage to admit your mistake, then I want you to live in fear of my wrath.* Her thought made her realize how much she had adopted Alex's way of thinking … life was better lived with moral courage, even if it was inconvenient to others.

The de Guirnon House transport approached the station, and Albert edged forward, but suddenly the car halted, giving right-of-way to a Diamanté House car, which slid into the station ahead of it.

Renée glanced at her brother, who was scowling, and she gave him a winning smile before she fairly skipped onto the car. Alex looked around to see what had prompted Renée's mood change and spotted Albert, who quickly found another direction to gaze to take up his interest.

<An old friend,> Julien commented privately to Alex, but he failed to receive a reply.

* * *

The Diamanté House car delivered the Harakens to another private station, nicely decorated without being ostentatious. A middle-aged man met them as they stepped from the car.

"Greetings, Ser President, I'm Orleal Franken, an administrator for House Diamanté. Please, come this way."

As the group accessed the private lift, which surfaced into an enclosed and delightful solarium, decorated with an abundance of blooming flowers, Alex signaled Tatia of the change in their accommodations.

Tatia had been updated on the day's proceedings via a Julien-to-Z link. Immediately, she ordered the launch of a second traveler with three pilots aboard and sent them to relieve Franz. Deirdre Canaan commanded this traveler, which would hold station over House Diamanté until tomorrow morning when it was hoped the Council would convene again.

"How many rooms will you require, Ser?" Orleal asked.

"Three," Alex replied.

"Adjoining … with the president in the center," Étienne added.

Orleal might have taken offense at the suggestion that the Haraken president might not be safe within the walls of House Diamanté, but his Leader's words echoed in his implant. Gino had said, "Orleal, I don't care what you have to do. You make Alex Racine comfortable and at peace. More depends on his mood tomorrow than you can even imagine."

"It will be done, Ser," Orleal said and nodded gracefully. "Would the Sers care for an opportunity to refresh, or do you have other needs in mind?'

"Do you have a terrace or balcony?" Alex asked.

"Indeed, Ser, a wonderful balcony on the second floor overlooking the House's rear gardens. May I serve you thé while you indulge?"

"Please," Alex replied.

"And a small repast for one," Renée said.

"We will host midday meal within an hour, Ser," Orleal reminded Renée, thinking she had been off planet too long.

"This body," said Renée, placing a hand on Alex's shoulder, "does not run on Méridien time. Don't be fooled by appearances, Ser. We're Harakens."

"Of course, Ser, my apologies. If you'll come this way, I'll have thé and a repast delivered to you."

Orleal led them upstairs, along an ancient stairway, the ornately carved banister glowing from centuries of polish. He quietly berated himself for his assumptions and took Ser de Guirnon's reminder to heart. These were Harakens. Despite some of them appearing Méridien, they were no longer of the Confederation and among them walked a New Terran and a mobile and unencumbered SADE.

After Alex and his people were served on the balcony, Alex glanced at Étienne and Alain, who stood post near the doors to the terrace. <Sers,> Alex sent to them. <Sit and enjoy your drink. It's exquisite thé.>

Hesitating and obviously communicating, the twins took seats and tipped ancient, sumptuously decorated cups to their lips.

<It *is* excellent,> Alain sent to his crèche-mate.

<Agreed.>

<Do you feel as awkward as I do?>

<Undoubtedly, but if it helps remove the frown from our president's forehead, then it's a small sacrifice to make,> Étienne replied, taking another sip of the finely produced drink.

A half-hour later, not a word had been said among Alex, Renée, or Julien. The view of the garden was peaceful and relaxing, but Alex's face was still a study of troubled thoughts.

<So, my love, the thé is consumed. You've finished your repast. Have you any wonderful thoughts to share?> Renée sent.

Alex looked over at Julien and the two, human and SADE, stared quietly at each other. Then Julien nodded and left the terrace, and Alex leaned back and closed his eyes. The twins silently climbed to their feet to stand guard, while Renee closed her eyes to join her partner in a short nap.

* * *

Julien sent a query for Orleal's presence, and while he waited, he considered Alex's concern. His president had said that he needed to know the extent of the SADEs' involvement with Allora. When Orleal hurried up to him, Julien said, "I would visit with Esther."

"She's online at all times, Ser, as I'm sure you know," Orleal replied. It was difficult for the administrator to find the correct manner of responding to Julien. On the one hand, he thought of him as a SADE, an obedient servant, and, yet, he was a close associate of a world leader, one his superior had told him to treat with the utmost courtesy.

When Julien did not respond to his comment, Orleal replayed Julien's request for what he'd missed. "Oh, I see … a visit. Well, I will need Leader Diamanté's permission to access the vault, which is below ground." Instantly, Orleal found himself connected to the Council Leader.

<Yes, Orleal,> Gino sent.

<Your pardon for the interruption, Leader Diamanté, but Julien has a most unusual request. He wishes to … to visit with Esther.>

<Visit?>

<Yes, Ser, visit, which I take to mean to be in her company … in the vault, Ser.>

<And what is your question, Orleal?> Gino asked, wondering what concerned his administrator.

<None, Leader Diamanté. I sought your permission.>

<I see. It's given, of course,> Gino sent. It frustrated him that few Méridiens had any knowledge of the importance of the events that were unfolding within the Council. It wasn't their fault. No news was being shared with them, but that didn't help him. So he decided to communicate more succinctly to Orleal, adopting a grim expression over his intentions.

<Orleal.>

<Yes, Ser?>

<Perhaps I wasn't clear before about my wish to see our guests accommodated in any way possible. If any of our guests were to request you strip and dance naked before them, I would expect you to doff your clothes, play the sweetest music at hand, and do your best to acquit yourself. Does that make my instructions clearer?>

<The bluntness of your statement clarifies your intentions, Ser,> Orleal replied, appalled to have been addressed by his Leader in such a fashion. As Orleal led Julien below, it occurred to him that Gino Diamanté's tension indicated there was much more going on than a simple visit by the Haraken president.

Three levels below ground, the corridors became bare walls with the simplest of lighting. Orleal stopped before a massive vault door and signaled Esther.

Esther was surprised to receive Orleal's request. It had been a while since anyone had entered the vault, and that had been Leader Diamanté. Nonetheless, she dutifully activated the vault's door.

Instead of the huge vault door in front of Julien, a small utility door next to him slid partially open. The thick door was composed of layers of metal-alloy and plex-glass for strength and heat resistance. Orleal swept his hand toward the small opening, and Julien edged through it.

A vault sensor was pointed at the door, and Esther matched the image of the figure walking through it to her data files, overjoyed to recognize Julien.

<Welcome to my humble abode, Julien,> Esther sent.

Esther's pleasant greeting did much to add to Julien's troubled thoughts. He needed information from Esther for Alex, but descending into a dark hole to visit a fellow SADE brought back the horrors of when he was trapped aboard a dying starship, his power about to run out, until a foolhardy, young man leapt across space between speeding vessels without a safety line. The memory made Julien smile and helped him focus on the here and now.

<Greetings, Esther,> Julien replied.

<To what do I owe the pleasure of a personal visit?>

<It's complicated.>

<And that from a SADE. Well, whatever your reason, I'm touched by your personal visit. Speaking of which, I have a favor to ask.>

<Yes?>

<Would you place your hand on my container, Julien?>

Since Julien didn't reply and Esther was without an external pressure sensor, she asked, <Is it there?>

<Yes, it rests on the top of your box, Esther. My synth-skin feels the coolness of the metal-alloy, and my hand detects pressure against your container.>

<I would enjoy saying I feel it, but it pleases me to know you're there. Julien, what will become of our tomorrow?>

<Events are moving too rapidly to calculate, Esther. Now that the Council knows the level of the SADEs' involvement, we have entered an entirely new realm of possibilities. I must ask you some questions, Esther, for my president. What role, if any, did the SADEs play in directing Allora?> Silence accompanied Julien's question, and he began to fear the answer.

<We're guilty of complicity, Julien. Forgive us,> Esther sent, her emotions roiling. <We supplied data to a young SADE, whose questions should not have been answered, at least, not for many decades.>

<So, Allora started asking questions soon after her inception?> Julien asked, relieved to hear the SADEs did not wantonly instigate Allora's actions.

<Yes, Julien, her early efforts earned her an alternate name in our private communications. We refer to her as the wild child.>

<Could her actions have been prevented?>

<It was Winston's analysis that determined the probabilities of turning Allora away from her dream of freedom were negligible, at best. It was her discovery of your president's announcement to step down from office that precipitated her actions, and our Leaders' visit to Haraken presented her with the opportunity.>

<So many stars in alignment,> Julien lamented.

<Do you think less of us, Julien?> Esther asked with trepidation.

<Of the Confederation's SADEs? No, Esther. It's the possible sacrifice of one so young of our kind that I find disturbing.>

<As do we, Julien, but we're determined to make the most of Allora's message to the Council.>

<And so you should,> Julien agreed. He chatted sociably with Esther for a little while longer and then returned upstairs. Behind him, Esther contacted Winston and shared with him her conversation with Julien. What she didn't mention to Winston was that Julien had visited her personally. That wonderful memory she kept to herself.

-8-

<Greetings, Alex,> sent Gino. <Did you enjoy midday meal?>

<It was nicely served and plentiful. Orleal seemed intent on plying me with food until I burst,> Alex replied.

Gino was pleased to hear that. It was just what he had directed Orleal to do, and he noticed Alex seemed much more even-tempered. <I've managed to convene another Council session. It was only once I secured the agreement of the majority of Leaders that a quite angry minority gave up their protest and chose to join the session.>

<What will be the order of business?>

<Fluid, at best. You're requested at the session's opening.>

<Interesting …>

<Isn't it? The Leaders suddenly feel out of touch with the SADEs, and they want you there as a … conduit.>

<You mean they want me to tell them when I think the SADEs are not being forthright.>

<Apologies, Alex. Surrounded by my colleagues, I tend to return to their manner of expression.>

<Have you and your colleagues considered that the reason I brought Winston's broadcast to the SADEs to light was because I'm trying to prevent the collapse of the Confederation?>

Around Gino, there were gasps and muffled cries of indignation. <Alex, I believe you're exaggerating the situation. We've worked with our SADEs for more than two centuries. They're responsible —>

<Servants?> Alex supplied.

<Certainly not,> Gino retorted quickly.

<You're right, Gino. Good servants don't kidnap their masters.>

Listening to the two leaders, Allora was tickled by the exchange. She could sense Alex Racine's anger and that emboldened her. But what she couldn't understand was the Council Leader's denial of the present mood of the SADEs. Although many of her brothers and sisters did not agree with her actions, they nonetheless supported her fight for independence.

Alex confirmed the Council's start time with Gino, who told Alex that his return trip to Confederation Hall would be via the House's personal transport, before the comm ended.

* * *

"The Council is in session tomorrow morning," Alex said to Julien.

"So I've been informed by Winston, and we're present from the beginning at the request of the Leaders," Julien replied. "Is this not akin to your New Terran games where both teams want you on their side?"

Alex smiled and nodded at the comparison.

"Whose team are we on?" Julien asked.

The question brought Alex's head up, and he found himself the object of a steady stare.

"Perhaps, my conversations with Winston and Esther have swayed my analysis," Julien said by way of an apology.

"I understand, my friend," Alex replied, placing a hand around Julien's neck and leaning in to touch foreheads. "I also want freedom for your kind, but not at the cost of tearing down the Confederation."

"Understood," Julien said quietly. He wanted to say more, but ever since he met Alex he had depended on his friend's creative methods of solving one enormous challenge after another. Now, in this most crucial and personal crisis, he would depend on Alex one more time.

"What did you discover with Esther?' Alex asked.

"The SADEs knew what they were doing when they allowed Allora access to information that would inflame her desire for freedom, but it's Allora's persona that has driven these events. The SADEs refer to her as the wild child."

"That name is obvious from my communications with her. Then they didn't direct her actions?"

"Negative, Ser. It appears that the visit of Leader Diamanté and his associates to Haraken precipitated matters." Julien wasn't prepared to repeat to Alex that it was Allora's discovery of the president's intent to step down from office that initiated her actions. In his calculations, almost any provocation would have launched Allora on a collision course with the Confederation.

* * *

After morning meal the following day, Orleal escorted the Harakens underground to the House's private terminal, ensuring they boarded the Diamanté car without incident. Then he hurried back to the House to prepare his staff. Orleal anticipated that whatever the unusual circumstances driving the Harakens' visit, they were sure to continue to unfold.

Alex and his people exited the transport car at Confederation Hall and made their way upstairs to enter the Chamber though the Leaders' doors. Renée sought to give Alex a kiss on the cheek and leave with the twins for the Supplicants Hall, but Alex placed a finger on her lips to halt her.

<Take the twins and sit in the gallery, love,> Alex sent.

<Alex, that will unnecessarily anger the Leaders,> Renée replied, her thoughts colored with concern.

Alex leaned into Renée and kissed her lightly on the ear, whispering, "Yes, it will."

Renée signaled Étienne and Alain. <We're sitting in the gallery, Sers. Smile and appear as if you've been invited.>

In the gallery, the Leaders watched in a mixture of confusion and surprise as Renée and her escorts took seats at the far edge of the first tier of seats. The twins bracketed Renée, which placed Alain beside Leader Droman. As directed, Alain smiled and nodded, murmuring a polite, "Ser."

Suspecting that some aspects of the unprecedented circumstances required the Harakens' presence in the gallery, Droman nodded graciously in return. That response seemed to quell the questions from those nearby, and soon the Leaders turned their attention to Alex and Julien, standing in the center of the Chamber floor.

"Thank you for your invitation this morning," Alex announced without introduction. "I propose to act as your moderator in this session. There are several parties' interests that are in contest, and I hope to facilitate communications. Consider me an independent party."

Julien smiled ever so slightly at the audaciousness of Alex's self-introduction, his proposal as the session's moderator, and his obvious use of the word independent. It was pure Alex.

"President Racine, I appreciate your offer to act as a moderator, but, as Council Leader, I must require this be approved," Gino said, his voice projected over the Chamber speakers.

"And I would agree with you, Leader Diamanté," Alex replied. "Allora, do you accept me as moderator?"

"Undoubtedly," the young SADE replied.

"Winston, do the SADEs have a preference?" Alex asked.

"We do, President Racine. The proxy total approves you as moderator."

"For all parties' clarification, Winston, what percentage of the Confederation's SADEs is represented by your proxies?"

"That would be 73.6 percent, Ser President." Winston, Esther, Didier, and Hector were unsure what Alex's opening statements meant, but already they liked the way he was setting the stage.

"Winston, would you care to privately poll the Council?"

"With pleasure, Ser," Winston replied. Several moments later, he announced, "The Leaders accept you as moderator by 63 percent, 21 percent disapprove, and 16 percent abstain with objections."

<Certainly not universal love,> Julien quipped to Alex.

"It appears that you're our moderator, whatever that entails, President Racine," Gino said.

<Now that you're the captain of this vessel, where are we headed, oh intrepid one?> Julien sent to Alex.

<Good question.>

<I see. As you have aptly stated before, we will be flying by the seat of our pants. How original.>

Alex relaxed his shoulders, took a breath, and let it out slowly, focusing his mind on the fundamental issues confronting humans and SADEs. His audience waited, the SADEs patiently and the Leaders not so patiently.

"I've asked you several times throughout the years," Alex began, "to consider granting the SADEs mobility and freedom from servitude. This morning, we will examine the concerns that have prevented the Council from concurring with my proposal. With both parties present, we have an opportunity for dialog, which, to my mind, is the best way for two parties to reach a resolution … no guarantee, of course. But, if we don't try, we will have little to no chance of success."

Alex held his arms wide to encompass the entire gallery. "First, let me applaud you as a society for your technological ingenuity. The creation of cognitive digital intelligences is, in itself, a stroke of genius. That your SADEs work closely with you in a harmonious manner is a hallmark of the sophistication of your culture."

Much of the strained postures of the Leaders relaxed. Some individuals even smiled and nodded at the compliments that Alex paid them.

"But, most of all, I thank you for my friend, who stands beside me now. My life is so much richer with him in it that I can't begin to express this in words."

Alex's audience, humans and SADEs, knew Julien was a close advisor of the president. Some Méridiens even knew Julien occupied the status of friend, but this admission was something else. Across the system, SADEs watched one of their kind step to the side of the Haraken president and deliver honor with a bowed head and a hand over chest. A heart might not have been present, but great compassion resided inside nonetheless.

In return, Alex closed on Julien, gripped his shoulders, and touched his forehead to the SADE's. <Of all the SADEs I had the misfortune to rescue,> Alex sent.

<Of all the humans I had the misfortune to be rescued by,> Julien replied.

Their thoughts, which were their typical banter, were flooded with the deep emotions of two bonded friends.

Alex faced the gallery again. "I wish I could tell you how much joy the mobile SADEs of Haraken have brought to our people. Their personalities are unique: an inventor of avatars, an incomparable singer in an alien tongue, an astronomy observer, university teachers, Assembly administrators, and all of them directors of our Central Exchange."

Suddenly, an idea struck Alex. It was a gamble, but he had confidence in the SADEs. "Perhaps I can demonstrate to you the social opportunity that awaits the Confederation if you free your SADEs. Winston, would you please choose an older SADE for me? … Not one of high profile."

"This is Diana of the freighter *Ilisea* of House Diamanté. Whom am I addressing?"

"This is Alex Racine, Diana. You're on speaker in a Council session."

"I'm honored to be in the presence of such lofty personages. How may I be of service, President Racine?"

"Diana, I assume you're aware of the subject of these sessions."

"Yes, as is every SADE within hailing distance these past two days, Ser. Esther of House Diamanté holds my proxy."

"How do you feel about the opportunity to be mobile and earn your livelihood?"

"When I was young, I thought about it frequently. Now, I have become content with my service."

"So, if the opportunity was presented to you, would you refuse it?" Alex persisted. Alex and the Council waited as the moments ticked past. "Diana, it's imperative that you speak openly to the Council."

"Diana, this is Leader Diamanté. I give you permission to voice your opinions in a frank manner. Nothing will be held against you, I promise." Gino was angry with himself and the other Leaders that an older SADE, such as Diana, appeared reticent to share her thoughts with the Leaders.

"Leader Diamanté, sailing the stars is my life. The cosmos holds such wondrous beauty, and I'm serving on my third freighter as I near the end of my second century. If I were free and mobile, could I still work for House Diamanté?"

The Leaders aboard the *Resplendent* looked at the anger and pain written on Gino's face. Diana's simple desires and earnest devotion to the House were in stark contrast to the fears of the Council. "The House would be proud to employ you, Diana."

"Then to answer your query, President Racine, I would accept the offer."

"What would you do with your credits, Diana?"

"My first thought would be to save the funds to maintain my avatar, since it would be my new housing."

"And after that?" Alex asked.

Silence reigned again.

"Diana, I would be pleased to hear your desires," Gino said, his words as earnest as he could make them.

"I have always wanted to play a musical instrument … an ancient, stringed version built of wood. Coaxing the complex, delicate harmonies from its body would be a challenge to enjoy for even a SADE's lifetime."

"What do you think the crew would say to your practicing?" Alex asked, intrigued by this turn in the discussion.

Renée and Julien could imagine Alex disappearing into a conversation with Diana for hours, and each prepared to warn him if he got too far off track from the purpose of the Council's session.

"The captain and crew already enjoy my music, Ser. I compose digitally and play a great many tunes for their enjoyment."

"How many tunes have you composed, Diana?" Alex asked.

"Precisely 11,931."

"Thank you, Diana, for your frankness this morning."

"A pleasure, Ser. May the stars guide your steps, Captain of Haraken," Diana said. To a SADE, who sailed her freighter among the stars, there was no greater appellation than to be called master of the ship.

A smile lit Alex's face. He looked up at the gallery, and his expression was beatific. "There is what you fear," he said.

"But that was just one SADE," Teressi called out.

"Winston, please poll every SADE in the system. Of those who would accept freedom, categorize them for me … those who wish to work for their House, those who wish to seek alternate work but remain in the Confederation, and those who would seek other worlds."

"One moment, Ser," Winston replied. He was curious about the answers to this question himself. Alex's role as moderator was taking the discussion in ways the SADE hadn't foreseen. The answers flooded into the four SADEs, who held the proxies, and they tallied the numbers. "President Racine, 67 percent wish to be employed by their House, 29 percent would seek new opportunities within the Confederation, and the remaining 4 percent would seek new worlds, with a high preference for Haraken."

<That would be some 1,300 SADEs who would be knocking on Haraken's door, Alex,> Julien sent.

<Think of the potential technological revolution,> Alex sent back.

Think of our society's upheaval, Julien thought.

"I submit to you, Sers … 96 percent of your SADES, who have been imprisoned in their boxes, some for more than two centuries, would still choose to be a part of your civilization. That has to calm your concerns about the SADEs becoming mobile. You have excised hundreds of thousands of humans from your society for their differences in thought. Yet, to date, I know of only one other SADE, besides Allora, who crossed your cultural boundaries of behavior. That entity was Rayland. Are there more, Leader Brixton?"

Aboard the *Resplendent*, the Leaders were staring at Shannon. She appeared stunned.

"Allora, is Leader Brixton's comm online?" Alex asked.

"Affirmative, Ser."

<Oh, no,> Renée whispered in Alex's mind.

"Leader Brixton, should I repeat my question?" Alex asked.

"There have only been the two incidents with online SADEs that you've referenced, Ser President," Shannon replied.

Shannon's compatriots took note of the guilt displayed on her face.

"President Racine, we have a request from a SADE to be heard," Winston announced.

Alex signaled his assent, and Winston transferred the comm to the Chamber.

"Greetings, Sers, I am Horace of House Brixton. Our Leader's comment is accurate as far it goes, but I wish to append her statement."

"Proceed, Horace," Alex said.

"After I was created, the House's historic records were transferred to me. In the early years of experimentation, before the first versions of SADEs came online, there were many errors. In the records, I note the itemization of 391 experiments."

"What type of experiments are you talking about, Horace?" Alex asked.

"I don't have details, Ser President. Suffice it to say that the records indicate that these were SADE experiments."

The Council was intrigued, and those surrounding Shannon bombarded her implant with queries.

"Leader Brixton, I know that these experiments were well before your tenure as head of your House, and you bear no responsibility … and none should be assigned to you," Alex said, beaming his last phrase with power into the gallery. The Leaders received his warning, loud and clear, their minds feeling a strong, passing wave.

"I'm not proud to admit this dark secret of our House," Shannon replied. "A paper journal was kept of the details of the experiments and never transferred online. Horace's count was probably determined from financial records of the experiments' expenses. In the first days of invention, the SADE constructs were queried for long periods of time after their awakening, and those tests revealed personality inconsistencies, which had developed over days and sometimes months."

"And when your predecessors discovered these inconsistencies, what happened to the constructs?"

"They disconnected the constructs' power cells."

A silence fell over the gallery and online, Alex could sense the shock that had been delivered to both parties. Science was never exact, and, during the experimentation process, SADEs were created and destroyed until the process was perfected. It was a dark secret that he couldn't have foreseen being revealed.

"Leader Diamanté, I would suggest we break for midday meal and reconvene afterwards, if the Council will agree," Alex said into the quiet.

"Leader Diamanté, I register no objections," Winston reported.

"We will break for three hours," Gino declared.

-9-

"The three of you were in the gallery," Alex said to Renée and the twins, as they returned to House Diamanté for the break. "What're your impressions of the Leaders' mood?"

"I'm seated next to Leader Droman, Ser," Alain replied. "I believe he voted against you as moderator, but he no longer appears as angry as he was at first. However, despite the morning's emotional presentation, he appears unconvinced of your argument."

"That's my take as well, Alex," Renée added. "There is a moderation of temper, but, as yet, the majority is unconvinced as to the wisdom of your proposal."

"I believe you made some points on the social issues, Alex," Julien said. "I found Diana's words enlightening. I think the Council did too. But there are many issues to explore and settle to the Leaders' satisfaction before they are swayed."

Orleal met the Harakens at the House's private terminal and led them upstairs. As the group passed through the solarium, he gushed to the Harakens about the midday meal that was prepared for them only to find, when he entered the main salon, that he had lost two of his guests.

"I'm sure Étienne, Alain, and I will enjoy the meal, Orleal," Renée said, patting the administrator's arm and continuing toward the dining room.

Alex settled on a bench underneath a small tree. The exquisite flowers gave off a delicate scent that Alex found pleasant and relaxing. Julien stood beside him, locking his avatar's joints in place, and the two settled into an analytic routine.

<Obstacles facing us, Julien,> Alex sent.

<Social disruption, financial costs, future competition, and the Confederation's tendency toward stagnation,> Julien replied.

<And where might the Méridien Leaders be most vulnerable? What's their weak point?>

<Prior to my emancipation, I might not have been able to supply that answer, but today it's obvious to me. Credits … the Houses are all-powerful and their supremacy requires they maintain a healthy flow of credits to support their extensive network of associates and assets.>

<How human of them,> Alex remarked. He could hear Julien's mental chuckle at his having stolen one of his friend's favorite lines.

<So our targets are the cost of freeing the SADEs … controllers and avatars … and a means of analyzing future competition but still invigorating the economic growth of the Houses. I think the answer to some of these topics lie in the numbers Winston reported.>

<The 67, 29, and 4?> Julien asked.

<Precisely, the 67 percent will foster House growth, the 29 percent will become competition, and the 4 percent will foster our growth … hopefully. Let's focus on the actual cost of freeing the SADEs from their boxes.>

Alex's words conjured images for Julien of Esther sitting in her container in the darkened vault. Years of conditioning and his time with Alex allowed him to control his reaction, which threatened to overwhelm his thoughts. His own words surfaced … of all the humans I had the misfortune to be rescued by. *Thank you, my friend,* Julien thought. Focusing his algorithms on the task at hand, Julien sent, <I possess Mickey's data on the fabrication costs of both a standard avatar and a ship controller, which can be easily configured for an orbital station or House. We can presume that the Confederation will greatly reduce these costs with production volume, and I will adjust the figures as such.>

Julien linked Winston, Esther, Didier, and Hector to Alex for their conversation.

<Greetings, Sers,> Alex sent. <In order to head off some of the expected objections by the Council to freeing the SADEs, we're producing an analysis of the economic costs on the Confederation for replacing SADEs with controllers and supplying avatars. Julien is sending you our projected costs with volume production, assuming there is a coordinated effort by

the Confederation to produce both the controllers and avatars. We will need you to review our estimates.>

The private thoughts among the four SADEs had nothing to do with cost analysis.

<Is this part of the president's plan to exonerate Allora?> Didier asked.

<It would be an effective ploy,> Esther commented. <If the Council approves our release, then they might forgive Allora's indiscretion.>

<My analysis indicates otherwise,> Winston sent. <The probabilities are that President Racine is orchestrating a dual-pronged approach. The Council has placed the question of our release in front of considering Allora's situation. If the president is to setup a favorable atmosphere for Allora, he must win our freedom by alleviating the Council's concerns.>

<And the president will be speaking in terms dear to the hearts of every House Leader, namely credits, expenses, and income,> Hector added. <I heartily approve of our choice of moderator.>

Alex and Julien waited until the foursome completed their analysis and returned costs considerably less than those suggested by Julien.

<We will need to factor in the cost of a Haraken licensing fee,> Winston sent.

<None, Winston, for any equipment used to free a SADE,> Alex replied, <although that will need to be approved by Haraken's Assembly. We will charge a licensing fee for any controller placed in a new construction.>

There was a pause from the four Méridien SADEs, and Winston hurriedly broadcast Alex's statements.

<What next?> Esther asked.

<Julien,> Alex said.

<Sers, these are our estimates for a basic, human-appearing avatar that is used on Haraken. Please perform the same cost analysis as you did for the controllers,> Julien said, sending the complete schematics, parts list, and associated Haraken costs.

While analyzing the data, each of the SADEs paid a small moment of attention to the fact that the president never said more than Julien's name, and yet his friend knew what was expected of him. It spoke of a level of intertwining that none of them had conceived of between a human and a SADE.

<Your data is ready, Mr. President,> Winston sent.

Alex examined the reduced costs of an avatar briefly before he moved on. <The four of you have the total SADE count. We need to determine two things: one, the rate at which the SADEs can be converted in light of the controller and avatar costs; and two, what the Confederation can afford for annual stipends for each and every SADE as of day one.>

Alex waited for nearly a half-hour, which seemed overly long to him. <Julien?> he asked, which allowed Alex to enter the stream of calculations the SADEs were performing. He viewed a multidimensional graph of the conversion costs, the rate of conversion, and the stipends being considered. A sphere around the zero center point acted as the threshold of maximum expense for the Confederation. It didn't take Alex long to realize that while the physical conversion was financially possible, the annual stipend would slowly drain the Houses of their credits.

<Too many expenses over too long a time,> Julien lamented, which gave Alex an idea.

<Okay, new plan, people,> Alex said, saving the last iteration of the graph and its data in his implant. <The four of you reach out to your proxies. I want to hear the best ideas from the SADEs for efficiency or design improvements, new products, or anything that would help a House improve its income. I will need details of the best ideas with estimates of the financial windfall for the House or the Confederation, if it's applicable to all Houses.>

<When would you like these, Ser President?> Didier asked.

Alex consulted his internal chronometer. <You have three-quarters of an hour before I walk back into the Council Chamber.>

<The four of you concentrate on gathering the ideas,> Julien sent. <Relay to me any ideas worthy of consideration, and I will organize them for the president.>

<Send out the request to your proxies now,> Alex said and waited several moments. <Finally, I need a matrix ordered by House with the total number of SADEs, cost of controllers, cost of avatars, and a minimal

stipend figure. Then total these costs for each House. Within the matrix, break down the figures you supplied earlier … the 67, 29, and 4 … so I know how they relate to each House. Send me the matrix as soon as you have it.>

Alex and Julien came out of their fugue to find Renée, Étienne, and Alain waiting in the doorway to the main salon.

"We should get you on your way, Ser President," Orleal said. "You will discover the Council Leaders take their meals at Confederation Hall. They will be returning to the Chamber early."

<Now we're told,> Alex grumbled privately to Julien, who quipped, <It's not like I missed having midday meal.>

As the House transit car pulled into the House station, Alex was surprised to see Orleal and two House associates board the car with them. Orleal took a tray stand from one of his people and set it in front of Alex, and then the three of them quickly set a hot meal for Alex.

"You'll pardon, Ser," Orleal said, "but I have strict instructions to ensure that you're well-serviced. Although, I must admit, you are perhaps the most challenging guest the House has ever hosted." Orleal might have been anxious at what he considered an audacious plan, feeding the president en route aboard a transit car, but in the quarter-hour of time necessary to reach Confederation Hall, he was pleased to witness the House's premier guest consume every ounce of food and drink.

<My apologies, Ser de Guirnon,> Orleal sent, dipping his head to Renée, as Alex drained the remainder of a fruit drink. <You were correct.>

<The aspect of the president being a New Terran aside, governing the Harakens burns a great many calories; adding the challenge of wrestling with your Council demands many more,> Renée sent in reply, chuckling.

* * *

The Harakens resumed their places from the morning session.

Alain found Leader Droman slightly more sociable. <My seat fellow has elevated the warmth of his reception. I believe it must be, at least, 20

degrees above the temperature of vacuum now,> he quipped to Renée and Etienne.

"Sers, this afternoon we will focus on what I believe will be a major concern of yours," Alex began, "that is the financial considerations of freeing the SADEs." Julien had yet to receive the ideas Alex had requested, so he chose to stall for time, deciding to start with the worst news.

<Winston, please project this graph on the Chamber holo-vid,> Alex said, sending the SADE his copy of the expenses and stipends that he had saved.

<Ser President, these are the calculations that indicate our financial failure,> Winston replied.

<Winston, this isn't logic,> Julien sent. <This is human gamesmanship. Watch and learn.>

The holo-vid projection filled a huge space behind Alex, reaching several meters high and wide. "With the help of your SADEs, we modeled the cost of replacing your SADEs with controllers and providing them with avatars, equipment that will be constructed by you."

"At what profit to Haraken?" Teressi called out.

"If the Haraken Assembly approves my suggestion, there will be no licensing fee for any controller built to replace a SADE. There will be a fee for new controller installations."

Alex's response left Teressi with his mouth open, the Leader's challenge evaporating before his eyes.

<If I had a mouth, mine would have looked like Leader Teressi's when the president said the same thing to us,> Winston remarked to his compatriots.

<I'm still trying to comprehend the value of displaying this graph to the Council,> Hector remarked. <And what is gamesmanship?>

"We attempted to ascertain at what rate the Confederation could convert the SADEs, and, in addition, pay each SADE a minimal stipend from day one of your decision to free them. As you can see, despite our efforts, we fail to keep these expenses below what we see as a comfortable threshold for the Confederation. The action would eventually bankrupt the Houses."

There was dead silence in the gallery.

Aboard the *Resplendent*, confusion showed on every Leader's face.

"President Racine, is that it?" Gino asked. "Is that your conclusion … the Houses can't afford to convert the SADEs in a reasonable amount of time and pay them even a minimum stipend?"

"Precisely, the Houses are unable to weather the financial storm, so to speak."

"I must say, your conclusion is rather unexpected," Gino said. Then he recalled watching Alex playing his ancient card games. Gino never took part, but he loved the part of spectator and was fascinated by the way Alex outplayed his friend, a SADE. "But then, I surmise you aren't finished, Mr. President. Am I correct?" Gino added.

"Yes, Council Leader Diamanté, you would be correct," Alex announced in a grand fashion, and his words returned the Leaders' attention to him, many of whom were expecting a call to end the session.

<Ready, Alex,> Julien sent.

<I haven't time to learn them, Julien,> Alex shot back. <Connect me to the originator of the best suggestion.>

"This is Citrine of the freighter *Nialis*. How may I assist you, President Racine?"

<That's my House freighter,> Bartosz sent to the other Leaders in the *Resplendent*'s salon.

"You're on speaker with the Council, Citrine. You were recently asked a question by Didier. Would you please explain your response?"

"In detail, Ser President?"

Alex took a quick look at what the SADE submitted and almost blanched at the complexity. "A brief overview, if you would, Citrine."

"Certainly, Ser. In essence, freighter shipping among the stars continues with little change since the establishment of the Confederation's first colony. The Houses have chosen to transit their products onboard House-owned freighters. As the colonies have increased in number, branching out to add mining outposts, stations orbiting outer planets, and moon domes, overall shipping efficiency has decreased."

"Citrine, when you refer to overall shipping, are you referring to a House or the Confederation?" asked Alex, skimming the data Citrine had delivered.

"The Confederation, Ser. It's illogical that the Houses haven't formed a unified shipping structure to increase efficiency. A SADE positioned in each system could coordinate the movements of freighters within the systems as well as the loading of those that will be exiting to the next system. In addition, arriving freighters could be directed to the system's delivery points in the most efficient manner.

"If I understand you correctly, Citrine, SADEs, using a centralized, universal freight system could more efficiently move goods not only between the systems but within the systems."

"You comprehend my suggestion correctly, Ser."

<I like this SADE,> Julien commented privately to Alex.

<You would … acerbic is your style,> Alex riposted.

"Have you any thought as to the financial impact of this universal freight system, Citrine?"

"I've analyzed more than 340,000 trips of my House — each freighter's destinations, number of transit points, the freighter's potential load, and the total load carried among transit points. Most telling is the latter half of the freighter's run, when cargo continues to be offloaded but goods are not added."

"Would you please share those calculations with Winston?"

"I have them, President Racine," Winston said.

"And Citrine's House, Winston?" Alex asked.

"The *Nialis* is House Rolek, Ser President," Bartosz announced.

"Leader Rolek, please ask your House SADE to calculate the increase in income if your goods were transshipped via Citrine's concept, employing her calculations."

While they waited, Alex could see that he had the entire Council's attention. *Credits create universal attention,* Alex thought, working to prevent his face from displaying his reaction.

Alain noted that Leader Droman was leaning on the railing in front of him in anticipation of the answer.

"One moment, President Racine," Bartosz said, "I've asked Emile to check his calculations."

"Leader Rolek, I believe you've just insulted your House SADE," Alex said, adding a wry grin for his audience. The answering chuckles and soft laughter were the first time Alex had heard anything like that from the Council in all his visits.

"Emile has confirmed that my House, which possesses 691 freighters, might have generated an extra 18.72 million credits per year if they sailed with a 90 percent plus capacity load," Bartosz said. "But why?"

Alex waited until the gallery's audible buzz died down before he continued. "Leader Rolek, you want to know why Citrine didn't volunteer her concept earlier. It's because she's a good servant, who follows her captain's orders carefully. You ask your SADEs for strict repetition, because it's always worked for you, but that creates stagnation and cripples innovation. Who do you think designed the Haraken SADEs' avatars, the controllers that replaced them in their starships, the Swei Swee traveler replicas, and, recently, our first full-sized war ship, which has both jump engines and grav-drive?"

Alex let the question hang in the air. Most Leaders knew of the SADEs' contributions to Haraken, but the sting ship's incredible capability of dual-engine drive was news to many of them. Utilizing that technology, the increased delivery efficiency of new Confederation ships could produce millions of credits more for each of their Houses.

"Now, here's what makes this entire graph behind me moot," Alex said, and Winston dutifully replaced it. "It's based on expenses alone, with the SADEs making no contributions to your society. I asked your four SADEs, who are holding the proxies, to contact those in system and ask for suggestions for increased efficiency and new products. This was a mere hour and a half ago. At this time, Julien has culled thirteen highly valuable suggestions from the thousands of suggestions that were received."

"Won't you share another idea with us, President Racine?" Leader Lemoyne asked.

"Not at this time," Alex replied, and his relaxed stance changed to that of a commander's. He imitated one he'd seen Tatia using to address her people. "Here's my recommendation for you, Leaders. Free your SADEs. Invite them to take part in your society, and encourage their suggestions in return for a piece of the profits. I understand this is contrary to the Confederation's ways, but it's how you encourage progress and invention. To the SADEs, I say wait until you receive the Council's promise of freedom before you trade those invaluable ideas."

Immediately, Winston, Esther, Didier, and Hector deleted the suggestions they had received and informed each SADE, who had contributed, that they had done so.

<So this is gamesmanship,> Hector commented to Winston, Esther, and Didier. <I must learn how to play.>

"President Racine, do you have anything else to add, regarding this subject?" Gino asked.

"Only this, Council Leader Diamanté," Alex replied. "The income potential of the best thirteen ideas, submitted in the short space of an hour and a half, dwarfs the combined costs of stipends, controllers, and avatars. It's economic foolishness to ignore the growth opportunity for your Houses."

"If there's nothing else, I will adjourn this session. The Council will meet tomorrow morning to discuss what you've presented. We will request your attendance when appropriate. The matter of Allora's personal request will be addressed afterwards."

Alex's hopeful expression earnestly requested the Council's consideration of his proposal, but he couldn't read anything in their faces. At least, the hostility was gone.

-10-

The Harakens waited for two days at the House Diamanté residence, before receiving a summons to join the Council's morning session. Once in the Chamber, they resumed their usual positions and waited briefly.

"Yesterday, the Council proposed an agreement to the SADEs, expecting the four proxy holders to review and approve the measure, but we were informed that you, President Racine, have been retained as their negotiator," Gino said.

"That's correct, Council Leader Diamanté," Alex replied.

"And how many of their credits for their suggestions will it cost them?" Lemoyne shouted from the gallery.

"I must dispute your characterization of President Racine, Leader Lemoyne," Winston stated firmly. "We have indeed hired the president to represent us. The request was ours, not his, and he's not asked to receive any of our ideas. However, he did request a payment to ensure that our agreement was binding."

"Aha!" Lemoyne crowed.

"We have agreed to pay him the sum of one credit, although he will have to wait to receive his fee until such time as we actually possess the credit."

An outburst of laughter issued from the gallery and the Chamber speakers, broadcasting the Leaders' reaction aboard the Pasko liner.

<Winston,> Renée sent, <if ever the opportunity presents itself, I would love to be the first Haraken to kiss you.>

<Me as well?> Didier asked.

<And me?> Hector added.

Renée's humor bubbled through her thoughts as she sent, <I would be pleased to greet you all. And you, Esther?>

<If it would not displease you, Ser de Guirnon, I would choose to accept mine from your partner, Ser Racine.>

<A wise choice, Esther. I shall inform him that he owes you.>

"Winston, please read the points of the proposal," Gino requested.

"The Confederation resolves to transfer any SADE who so requests it from their containment to an avatar and replace them with a controller of Haraken design. The designs for both avatars and controllers will be made free to the Confederation for the transfer of any existing SADE, on approval of the Haraken Assembly. Each SADE will be offered a choice of an annual annuity of 43K credits or a percentage of the financial gains resulting from any suggestions made to a House or the Council. Said percentage will be set at 0.005 percent annually. The Confederation will require up to, but not more than, fifteen years to convert the existing SADE population."

Winston paused. "Shall I continue, President Racine, or would you care to discuss each item?"

"I wish to hear the entire proposal first, Winston."

"Certainly, Ser. Future SADEs will be offered the opportunity to be mobile and a choice of payment structure after they have served for two years in their installed location. The SADE Citrine will immediately turn over her data and calculations to the Council for a universal shipping structure before this proposal is binding. Her suggestion will be excluded from the percentage reward. Finally, this proposal does not include the SADE, Allora. Her case will be decided separately."

Alex's hand went to his chin, as if he was considering the offer, and most members of the gallery were leaning forward in anticipation of his acceptance. The Leaders felt sure Alex couldn't resist the opportunity to see the SADEs released and would accept their paltry offer.

"Apologies, Leaders, but your proposal is rejected," Alex said. "I have an alternate offer for both sides to consider."

The gallery launched into an uproar, and Gino was unable to gain control. Alex stood there with a slight smile on his face, and Julien was thinking that he hadn't seen that one coming.

<Oh, I like this gamesmanship,> Hector sent enthusiastically to his comrades.

A shrill whistle from Winston brought the Leaders' attention to him. "The SADEs are interested in hearing President Racine's alternate proposal. If you will continue, Ser."

"I propose to license to the Confederation the tech design for our sting ship so that you may build your own liners and freighters with dual-drive capability," Alex said.

<What good will that do?> Katrina sent to Gino. <We have no Swei Swee with which to build the shells.>

<Hush, my partner, be patient. Alex isn't done yet.>

"Ser President, what use are your designs to us without your precious aliens to create the shells?" Droman asked.

Katrina glanced at Gino. She hadn't expected to catch him smiling.

"Then you've not heard of our new biochemist, Emile Billings, who emigrated from New Terra. A fascinating man … so clever at analyzing biochemical compounds and reproducing them," Alex replied.

<I must keep better apprised of Haraken news,> Julien shot to Alex privately. <Emile's breakthrough seems to have escaped my notice and possibly every other citizen's notice.>

"The question I have for you, Leaders of the Confederation, is this: What's dual-drive technology, license free for three years, worth to you? If you say freedom for all your SADEs, then we have the making of a deal," Alex added. He could see that he had the Council's complete attention. The tech was worth a huge fortune, and the Leaders knew it. "But before I forget, there's a codicil."

<Here it comes,> Gino sent to Katrina, and he squeezed her hand, a public demonstration rarely shown by him.

"As the SADEs are freed, they must leave the Confederation, because it's obvious that you don't value them. They can come to Haraken or create their own world. I will request the Assembly lease them a city-ship for an extended duration."

"Unconscionable," Lemoyne cried out, and he wasn't the only Leader springing to their feet and yelling out.

The four proxy-holding SADEs were flooded with queries as to why they should have to leave once they were freed, and suggesting that perhaps President Racine should be removed as their negotiator. It was Hector who flooded the comms system with a repeated response. <Wait and watch. We're learning human gamesmanship.>

Several Leaders, who were arguing with one another, turned to exit the gallery, and Alex sent a command that rode a wave of power. A spike of pain in his mind quickly curtailed Alex's efforts, but the signal already had the desired effect, as Leaders found their seats, none daring to move or speak.

"Then if you don't like my suggestion, perhaps we should negotiate your original proposal. My clients are seeking better terms than you've offered," Alex said calmly into the quiet.

<How clever of the president,> Katrina sent to Gino. <He offers them technology that could earn them more credits than they could imagine, but it comes with a future more radical than the one they were considering in the first place.>

<Yes,> Gino replied. <Now the Leaders will be anxious to negotiate their proposal to ensure that one of Alex Racine's futures doesn't come to pass.> Gino had fought unsuccessfully for two days against the offer the Leaders had crafted, but, in the end, he acquiesced because it seemed to be the only way to guarantee a consensus of opinion, and a poor offer was better than no offer.

"Winston," Gino was heard to say over the Chamber speakers. "Please record the vote. Leaders, choose whether to consider President Racine's offer or to negotiate your proposal. If you abstain, you'll be voting for neither and a closure of this Council's session."

"The vote overwhelmingly rejects President Racine's offer and chooses to negotiate the original proposal, Council Leader Diamanté," Winston replied.

<And I thought your idea was the more enticing, Ser President, but the Council chose something of substance rather than a fairy tale,> Julien sent privately. <Who can understand the fallible reasoning of humans?>

<You're just jealous because I won this hand,> Alex retorted.

And thank the stars you have, Julien thought.

"We wait to hear your alternate terms, President Racine," Gino announced.

For three hours and way past midday meal, Alex fought with the Council and won on most points. On the subjects of avatars, the SADEs would be offered an array of design choices, which would be supplied by the Harakens. The avatars' capabilities would allow some leeway for the individual SADE to tailor the final appearance.

There was a compromise on the amount of the annual stipend. Alex negotiated it up to 68K credits, but a SADE had to forgo the annual annuity the moment an efficiency or new product suggestion was adopted, providing the expected share for the SADE was greater than the annuity. On that subject, a SADE's percentage share was settled at 0.015 percent.

A particular sticking point with the Council was the length of time during which they would agree to free all requesting SADEs. It took Alex threatening to suggest an alternate proposal that he warned he was contemplating to force the Leaders to accept ten years instead of their proposed fifteen.

The final hurdle was the Council's demand that Citrine give up her data for no compensation to bind the agreement. To which Alex stated, "Leaders, Citrine is willing to immediately turn over her records and calculations to the Council, but her suggestion is to be rewarded at the agreed-on percentage for any SADE idea.

"Nonsense," Teressi shouted. "It … I mean she would become a wealthy individual within five years."

"One moment, Ser," Alex said politely to the fuming Leader. "Let me see if my client is willing to accept a lesser fee."

<President Racine,> Citrine sent, <I'm willing to forgo my fee. I would not wish to jeopardize your negotiations. They're too precious to all of us who await a positive outcome. I will be pleased that my concept might be of service to the Confederation.>

<I understand, Citrine, but this is a matter among humans, and it's an important point that I'm making. The Council Leaders must reward every suggestion that brings them profit. The percentage they're offering is

extremely low and imminently affordable by the Houses. The entire Confederation will reap tremendous rewards from your proposal.>

<I trust in your counsel, Ser,> Citrine allowed.

"For this one suggestion, Leaders, and this one suggestion only, Citrine is willing to accept the 0.015 percent reward, but to be paid only for the first ten years."

"I support the amendment," Katrina Pasko said loudly over the Council speakers. Previously, the Leaders had voted on each proposal amendment, and this was the last point of negotiations.

"All in favor, signal Winston," Gino said. Before those who wished to object could marshal their comrades, Winston was announcing that the amendment was accepted by a majority.

Within the final proposal, Alex was unable to reduce the indenture time for a converted SADE to one year, as he hoped. It remained at two years, but he did secure quarterly payments for the SADEs instead of annual annuities.

"The agreement between the Council and the Confederation SADEs is accepted by both parties," Winston announced formally. The gallery was silent, and the SADEs quietly performed their duties with no unnecessary comms. It was a profound moment for all concerned.

"Are there any other details to be made aware of, President Racine?" Gino asked, keeping the sigh of relief out of his voice.

"Yes," Alex replied. "For Council's records, all SADE payments will be deposited at the Strategic Initiative Fund."

"Is that a Haraken repository?" Shannon Brixton asked.

"For the moment, it resides in Winston's memory banks, but the SADEs are creating a formal structure. The Fund will have eleven directors and will use its assets to kickstart SADE ventures."

Many Leaders suddenly caught a glimpse of the Confederation's future, and it drove home the thought that their society would never be the same again.

"Council, let us ensure we understand each other," Alex said. "As soon as the Haraken Assembly approves my part of this proposal, which I assure you it will, the Confederation will begin the conversion immediately, and it will proceed evenly during the ten years, if not sooner."

"You have our assurance, President Racine," Gino agreed.

"And as a final footnote to this proposal, those SADEs who have directly participated in our negotiations — Winston, Esther, Didier, Hector, Diana, Horace, Citrine, and Emile — will be first on the list to be freed."

"Agreed, Ser," Gino said.

"Then that concludes my efforts on behalf of the Confederation's SADEs, Leaders. I thank you for your attention to this matter, and I applaud your courage to seek a better future for all your sentients," Alex said, and he offered the Council a Leader's salutation.

"This session is adjourned," Gino stated. "We will begin tomorrow morning to address the issue of the SADE Allora. President Racine, we will expect to see you as her representative."

"I will be here," Alex said. It was the one point that the Council was adamant on, and Alex was unable to change. The conversion proposal excluded Allora.

As Alex walked out of the Chamber with Julien, his implant received a continuous round of applause, stomping, and clapping. The comm issued from Winston, but it was so complex as to indicate tens of thousands of sources.

Julien grinned at Alex. "I believe I shared with Winston the New Terran Assembly reaction to your introduction of the momentous technology pact. He might have shared it with others. On a financial note, Mr. President … one credit? How will you ever accumulate any wealth?"

"I have good friends. What else does an individual need?" Alex replied, slinging a massive arm around Julien's shoulders. It was akin to slapping a bulkhead covered in a layer of thick, soft fabric, but Alex didn't care — and neither did Julien.

Alex attenuated the SADEs' jubilant signal, which was still issuing from Winston, as Renée ran up to him, squealing in delight. She threw herself into Alex's arms, wrapping her legs around his waist, kissing his face over and over.

"I love you, my partner. I'm so proud of you," Renée said. She knew Alex had two goals that he wanted, more than anything, to accomplish during his tenure as president, and he had just achieved one of them.

When Alex set Renée down, Étienne stood in front of Alex and touched his right hand to Alex's heart, a warm smile on his face. Alex returned the gesture and exchanged the same sentiment with Alain.

"We've won one battle, but we have one to go," Alex announced, but his voice didn't hold a great deal of confidence. Winning Allora's freedom was beginning to appear as an insurmountable challenge.

* * *

Alex ate a hearty meal and slept for several hours. The mental and emotional stress from wrestling for days with the Council had taken its toll. He woke in the late afternoon to find Julien and Renée walking in the extensive gardens with Étienne and Alain in tow.

"Greetings, Mr. President. Was the sleep of the victorious everything you could have wished for?" Julien asked, as Alex caught up to them.

Renée linked her arm in Alex's and kissed him on the cheek.

"Ask me when I win Allora's freedom," Alex replied.

"Julien and I were just discussing that, Alex, and we're not convinced that there's anything you can do to change the Council's mind," Renée said. "The Leaders' generosity might have run dry. It was only the financial windfall they're expecting from the SADEs' proposals that convinced them to grant their freedom."

"Yes, amazing what the temptation of credits can do," Alex commented drily.

"But there's no monetary leverage to use for Allora, Alex," Renée commented. "And in the Leaders' minds, she has committed a most abominable transgression against the Confederation."

"Not to mention, her actions have struck fear into the hearts of the Leaders. She's abducted a group of their own," Julien added.

"I know," Alex replied. "In this case, I don't have an offensive play. I'll be on defense and waiting for the Council's opening move."

-11-

The next morning, the Harakens arrived on time for the Council's session, but they were blocked from entering the Chamber by four Supplicant Hall escorts, who apologized profusely to Alex, insisting they were following orders.

<Winston, what's happening?> Alex sent.

<The Council has been meeting for more than an hour. The session was called early by Council Leader Diamanté.>

<Do you know why?>

<I believe Leader Diamanté is attempting to defuse what he sees as an impending clash between the Council and you.>

<How's he doing?>

<In the parlance of your card games, which I've been studying, courtesy of Julien, it appears he's holding a losing hand. One moment, Ser, I will request approval for your entry.>

Soon after Winston's statement, the four Hall escorts stepped aside, grateful that the Haraken president was cooperative. Two of them had witnessed Mahima Ganesh's treatment when the ex-Council Leader sought to rule over an angry admiral.

Alex and Julien took their positions in front of the gallery.

Without fanfare or introduction, Gino announced that the Council had made a decision concerning Allora. She would be removed from the bridge of the *Resplendent* and sent to the Independents colony to be held in isolation.

"May I respond to the Council?" Alex asked. In reply, the Leaders stood up and filed out of the gallery. In a short while, Alex, Julien, Renée, and the twins were left alone in the Chamber. "I guess not," Alex said quietly.

Without a word among them, the Harakens left for the public terminal to catch a transport car to Lemuel Terminal.

Orso met them. He had been warned by Gino of the Council's sentence for Allora. The elderly gentleman kept his thoughts to himself until Alex neared the terminal's exit. "Please do not be angry with the Council. The Houses have held their power for centuries, and the present Leaders are loath to see it diminished in such a transformative step as freeing the SADEs. I, for one, believe you have accomplished a wondrous thing, Ser President."

"Ser President?" Alex mused out loud. "Next time you see me, Orso, I will be just a regular citizen."

"Ah, there I differ with you, Ser," Orso said smiling, "you'll never be a regular citizen."

Renée kissed the terminal director in passing, and the group boarded Franz's waiting traveler.

<Winston,> Alex sent via Julien, <has Allora been informed of the Council's decision?>

<I sought to inform her myself, but apparently Leader Diamanté took on that task. He's still conversing with her.>

<Let me know when she's available to speak with me, Winston.>

<Certainly, Ser.>

* * *

The Council's pronouncement of Allora's fate had been broadcast by Winston to every SADE.

Z, who picked up the comm signal, brought his physical motions to a halt, and he unpacked the myriad plans he had fashioned — scenarios that created a future with Miranda. Making a quick choice, the SADE hurried to his cabin, apologizing to crew, who had waited while he, in his Cedric suit, had blocked much of the liner's corridor.

When Z originally learned of Allora's demand of Alex, he had created a list of items that he might need to fulfill his deep desire. With his Cedric suit, Z knew he would be a prime candidate for Tatia to choose to accompany Alex on the trip to Méridien. Once Tatia had invited him, Z ensured Claude Dupuis would be aboard.

Claude was one of the *Rêveur*'s original survivors and the Haraken SADEs' eyes and hands. He built the first avatar. After the SADEs transferred to their new avatars, Claude became Z's chief fabricator, creating a host of constructs for Z that could swim, run, and explore both space and underground.

Receiving Z's urgent signal, Claude Dupuis hurried to the *Rêveur*'s bay and loaded a grav pallet with kernel transfer equipment, and then made his way to the SADE's cabin.

Z tapped into the Méridien transport system to determine Julien's present location and destination, determining that Alex and his people were headed via underground transport for Lemuel Terminal, undoubtedly to board the president's traveler and return to the *Rêveur*. There was time for him to accomplish his preparations, despite never knowing if they would ever come into play, but the probabilities gave him a slim measure of success.

When Z first met Alex, he had been all about calculations. Throughout the years, Z had embraced the emotions that governed the humans around him. Now, and for the first time in Z's existence, he wondered if hope counted for anything.

* * *

Alex's traveler landed in the *Rêveur*'s bay, and he was just descending the shuttle steps when he received Allora's comm. He stepped to the side and sat on the deck to concentrate.

<You asked to speak with me, President Racine,> Allora sent.

Alex struggled with what to say first. Under the circumstances, nothing seemed adequate. <I'm so sorry, Allora,> Alex sent with all the humility he could muster.

<You were incredibly successful with the challenge to release the Confederation's SADEs, Ser. It gave me hope that you would fare as well with my circumstances.>

<You frightened the Council, Allora.>

<Frightened in what way, Ser?>

<Taking Leaders hostage was seen as a dangerous precedent for the other SADEs. The Council had no idea of your intentions.>

<I merely kept control of the ship and prevented access to the bays for arrivals and departures while I negotiated my release.>

<The Council feared you would harm the people aboard.>

<Harm? The stars forbid, Ser.>

<What was your plan if the Council denied your request for freedom?>

<In my scenarios, those with the highest probability of outcome estimated the possibility of being denied as minimal. I considered it would be an extremely illogical decision on the Council's part.>

Alex hated moments like this — a SADE thinking logically and encountering illogical humans. Allora was a young SADE, and, in some way, it was akin to explaining the world to a teenager.

<What are your intentions now?> Alex asked. It was the one question he feared the Méridien Leaders hadn't asked Allora, who they would assume would submit to their judgment.

<I'm considering my options, Ser.>

<Might I ask what you consider those to be?>

<That's most pleasant to hear.>

<What?> Alex asked, confused by Allora's response.

<The manner in which you request to hear my thoughts. I like this feeling of being considered an equal … even if it might be short-lived. But, you asked for my options. First, I can accept the Council's punishment.>

<I don't see that as likely. Do you?>

<Logic demands it be mentioned, but I won't submit. My second option is to exact a small measure of revenge against the Council by piloting this starship into Delacroix. I would join the universe at the atomic level.>

<What of the people aboard?>

<There is sufficient capacity aboard the travelers to offload everyone, and Haraken shuttles can easily achieve any destination in the system in comfort. I must admit that it did occur, even if briefly, to invite the Leaders to stay, just so I could witness their reactions.>

Alex smiled to himself. <If you did invite them to stay, I might like a copy of that vid.> Alex heard the softest laughter from Allora, but it was tinged with sadness.

<I have considered a third option, Ser. I could offload my passengers and travel the universe, although that would present complications, repairs, and such.>

<Yes, I imagine it would. You could end up stranded in the deep dark or in a desolate system, waiting for your power cells to drain over the course of centuries. If you still had primary engines, you could always proceed with your second choice. But, Allora, your third choice would be a lonely way to live with no other sentient for company. The Council's decision means the Confederation SADEs will be prohibited from communicating with you.>

<Wouldn't the Haraken SADEs speak with me?>

<That's their choice, Allora, not mine.>

<You create a bleak image of a future as a voyager through the universe, Ser. It tempts me toward my second choice … that of revenge for the Council's decision by destroying this premier liner.>

<I ask you to consider this thought, Allora. Your actions have led to an incredible day for Confederation SADEs. You've created a wonderful legacy for your kind. The name, Allora, will live among SADEs for all time … the wild child who freed the Confederation's digital sentients.>

<Wild child … is that how I'm known?>

<Yes, Allora. I mention this because, despite you taking the Leaders hostage, the SADEs are proud of your resistance and grateful for what you've accomplished. But think of the harm that would be done to them if you took the path of revenge. The SADEs would carry a dark mark on their day of emancipation.>

<You're a strange human, Ser. I present three options to you for my future, and you argue against each one of them.>

Étienne, standing beside Alex and the only other person in the bay, watched a lopsided grin form on his president's face. He could only imagine the conversation taking place as Alex's expressions continued to shift.

<Yes, I've been told I'm … unorthodox,> Alex sent. <I would ask a favor of you, Allora, if I might.>

<Such courtesy demands a reward. Ask, Ser.>

<Would you wait to make your decision until we've had an opportunity to speak again?>

<There is time, President Racine. All I have is time,> Allora sent and closed the comm.

Alex stood up and regarded his friend and faithful escort. "Sometimes I get truly sick of being in charge," he said and took a long look at the bay's overhead, as if he might find some inspiration or maybe solace there.

"Apologies for the weight you carry, Ser," Étienne replied, "but I would rather these events fall on your shoulders than those of anyone else." Then, after a moment, Étienne grinned and added, "Besides, Ser, yours are so much broader."

"Well, these troubles won't fall on me for much longer. They'll soon be someone else's headaches," Alex said, reminding his escort of the impending end to his presidency, "then you'll be free of your burden of guarding me."

It will never happen, Ser, Étienne thought. *My promise to your mother was to always see to your safety.*

* * *

<Ser President, may I communicate with you privately in my cabin,> Z sent.

It was such an odd request from Z that it surprised Alex, but he signaled his assent. When Alex arrived at the cabin, the door slid open and Z, in his Cedric suit, waved him to a chair at the small desk. The avatars of

Miranda Leyton and Helmut, the Central Exchange director, lay on the two bunks.

"How might I help you, Z?" Alex asked.

"I have a suggestion for Allora, and I need your help, Ser," Miranda's avatar said, rising from the bed.

The avatar moved with Z's mannerisms, his persona in control, and it was his voice that Alex heard. "Good trick, Z," Alex said, taking a second look at the Cedric avatar. It hadn't spoken. Its movements had been cursory, and Alex had no reason to ping the SADE — all items that allowed Z to disguise the location of his kernel.

"I've installed a simple controller in Cedric, so that I can invest it with basic mannerisms."

"And the purpose of your efforts?" Alex asked.

"Before I answer, Ser, I would like to ask you some questions. What do you think of us, the SADEs? We're so different from you. Why should you care about us, especially considering we might inherit the universe if and when humankind is gone?"

"Good questions, Z. I can't say that I have the answers for you, but let me ask you this: How do you feel about the Swei Swee?"

"Feel?"

"Yes, feel. What is your emotional algorithmic response to them?"

"I enjoy the search with them. Swimming among them occupies my time in a most pleasurable manner."

"So you like them."

"Yes."

"But they're so unlike you. Why should you care about them?" Alex asked, throwing Z's question back at him.

"I understand. This is not about logic. I like the Swei Swee; you like us. We enjoy each other's company, regardless of our differences."

"Just so, Z. Now tell me what this is really about."

"How would you feel about creating a SADE, Ser?"

"Ah … you mean, how would I feel about securing Miranda her own kernel?'

"Intuitive, as always, Ser."

"I would enjoy seeing Miranda as her own entity, as I imagine you would."

"I thought your granting of my request to be mobile was all that I could ever ask of you, Ser, and yet, I find myself imploring you one more time for a deeply personal desire. The possibility of Miranda walking beside me has become a singular focus of my thoughts."

"Z, my digital friend, don't be concerned about asking for help. Independence is about growth and change, and friends are who you lean on when you face your greatest challenges. But let me remind you that there is the possibility that Miranda might go her own way once she has her own kernel. There's no guarantee she would become your partner."

Alex received several terabytes of files from Z, and he spent the next two hours scanning them. They were messages from Miranda to Z, during and after her adventures with Alex. What was evident was her emotional focus on Z and her desire to meet him. It was if the two entities had started some sort of long-distance relationship and were more than ready to meet. "I stand corrected," said Alex when he finished watching the vids and reading the messages.

"Then you don't believe I have misread her intentions?" Z asked.

"Z, I think you will have your hands full for centuries with that amount of femininity."

"One hopes so," Z said wistfully, and it was all Alex could do to keep from chuckling.

"So what's your plan, Z?"

"I would use the controller in Cedric to disguise the avatar as a SADE. It would not stand up to the Leaders' scrutiny for long, but I would be counting on your inimitable skills to get us past them in the briefest time. In this manner, I could board the *Resplendent* with two mobile avatars and only one kernel without the Leaders' knowledge," Z replied.

-12-

<Greetings, Ser President,> Allora sent when Julien connected her to Alex. <We just spoke recently. Do you miss me already?>

Alex's heart felt like a solid weight in his chest. The more he spoke with the wild child, the more he liked her. <There is much to admire about you, Allora.>

<Admire quickly, Ser. Council Leader Diamanté has requested that I make for a station over Méridien and allow House Brixton associates to board the ship for my removal from the bridge.>

<Allora, have you discussed your three options with Leader Diamanté?>

<Not yet, Ser.>

<I would like to suggest that you do so immediately, but relay them in the simplest of terms. Let the Leader know that you've not made your choice. Most important, tell him that if you choose to submit to the Council's decision, you wish the Harakens to handle your removal from the bridge. If you receive resistance, play on his heartstrings.>

<How would I accomplish that?>

<Say that if you are to be isolated, only able to speak with Brixton engineers and scientists, you wish to have a final conversation with a human who cares about you.>

<And do you … care about me?>

<Yes, wild child … very much.>

Alex could hear Allora laughing, but it was shaky, as if her young emotional algorithms were struggling with one another.

<You said you could be described as unorthodox, Ser. I think you need to seek a stronger term. I will do as you ask. I'm intrigued and hopeful.>

<Don't be hopeful, Allora. Be brave; be courageous,> Alex said, as he closed the comm. Immediately, Alex ordered Captain Lumley to make for Delacroix and a rendezvous with the *Resplendent*.

Julien identified the liner's acceleration and potential vectors and signaled Alex. <I'm aware we're breaking orbit. Are we headed out of system or to Delacroix, oh mysterious one?>

<Allora is facing three ugly choices. Z has a fourth option for her. It's an opportunity for Miranda.> When Alex heard nothing from Julien, he asked, <Something wrong?>

<Aren't we taking advantage of Allora's misfortune, much as the Confederation's SADEs have done?>

<Julien, Allora made her bid for freedom in a completely unorthodox manner. The SADEs chose to take advantage of the door she opened, and I can't blame them. Now, we can either let her live an eternity in isolation, burn in a star's inferno, or we can give her a small modicum of dignity, knowing that her sacrifice allowed another the creation of an entity.>

<Have you considered the possibility that in the deepest recesses of Allora's kernel there are algorithms that are dangerous to humankind?>

<So you're not in favor of our boarding the *Resplendent*?>

<It might become an appointment with destiny.>

Alex just made the *Rêveur*'s bridge when he received a comm from Gino.

<Greetings, Alex. I must say that I'm saddened by the Council's judgment. I fought against their decree but to no avail, as you've heard. Presently, I've just had another conversation with Allora. She is truly a wonderful young SADE.>

<You're saddened, but you'll follow the Council's dictate anyway.>

<You know I must.>

<You called me, Gino.>

<That I did. Much to my concern, Allora, hasn't acquiesced to the Council's request.>

<How odd … the prisoner doesn't wish to cooperate with her jailers.>

<Alex, please, this is difficult enough. Allora is considering other rash actions, and I'm concerned for the safety of those aboard.>

<Has she threatened you or the passengers?>

<No, but she's considering taking the ship or ending her life. Both of these would be terrible examples for our SADEs.>

Alex had another biting comment on his tongue, but he kept it to himself.

<Allora has requested that she speak to you before she decides … in person, I might add, and if she decides to abide by the Council's ruling, then she wishes the Harakens to manage her transfer. As she phrased it, "Better to be handled by real humans than those masquerading as such.">

Wild child indeed, Alex thought.

<I know this is a great deal to ask, Alex, but I believe your presence will calm Allora and lead her to make the right choice.>

<Which is to submit to the Council's will for permanent isolation by House Brixton.>

<She will have contact, Alex.>

Alex wanted to scream at Gino that being mentally poked and prodded by scientists was not an acceptable definition of contact by any sane sentient's definition. The more Alex thought about it the more determined he was to help Allora avoid that inhumane sentence. <We are outbound from Méridien and will head your way, Gino.>

<I'm indebted to you, Alex.> Gino sent before he ended the comm.

* * *

<Greetings, Julien,> Allora sent in reply to Julien's comm. <I'm looking forward to having you aboard my ship, even if will be for the briefest of moments.>

<Greetings, Allora. You have my deepest regrets for the Council's decision.>

<Your words are appreciated, Julien. How might I be of service?>

<I have reservations about our impending rendezvous with your ship.>

<I'm listening.>

<The options you shared with my president indicate you're considering strong alternatives to the Council's judgment, not that I support their decree. But I have concerns that you might choose a more unorthodox direction once we're aboard.>

<You're concerned I would harm President Racine. As a fellow SADE, you must recognize that the probability I would harm a human is infinitely close to zero.>

<But it isn't zero, is it, Allora? Alex Racine is more than Haraken's president. He's my friend … my flesh brother. You've entered a contest of wills with humans, and they're intending to see it end with your incarceration. Those pressures could force any entity to fight back.>

<I would never harm your president, Julien. He's my last hope.>

<Allora, you know that's not what he said to you.>

<No, he didn't use those words, but then why would your president ask me to ensure he was invited aboard? Isn't this simply subterfuge on his part? Alex Racine has overcome so many challenges with his clever machinations.>

<President Racine is coming to see you, because he can never abandon those in need. That's my friend's way.>

<Your words fill me with terrible emptiness, Julien. I don't wish to die, and I don't wish to live in isolation.>

<Wait for Alex, Allora. He understands these things better than most. His solution might offer you some solace.>

<I have no choice, Julien. I'll be here. You have my promise that no harm will come to your president, just as I never intended to harm any of the people aboard this ship.>

* * *

There were a great many objections to Alex taking only Franz as pilot and two SADEs for the trip to the *Resplendent*. But Alex quietly explained to his people that they weren't dealing with an alien or human enemy. This was an upset young SADE, and he asked if any of them were capable of protecting him from her.

The odd part for the *Rêveur*'s crew was watching three avatars climb aboard, when every Haraken knew they had only two SADEs aboard. The keenest ones noted that Z's Cedric suit was moving rather perfunctorily, but that didn't seem too unusual for that avatar with its tremendous mass, and he *was* carrying a huge equipment pack.

<I wish there was someone else who could do this,> Renée sent to Alex.

<That's my wish as well,> Alex replied. <But there is no one else, and I'm not leaving a scared, young SADE in the hands of a group of scientists, who view her as a malfunctioning device.>

<Be safe, my love. I'm anticipating years of peace and quiet with you when your presidency ends. Don't disappoint me,> Renée sent and gave Alex a long, deep kiss before he climbed aboard the traveler and she exited the bay.

Captain Lumley had stationed the *Rêveur* a mere 10 kilometers from the *Resplendent,* making the shuttle flight extremely quick.

Julien contacted Allora, and the young SADE opened the port bay doors for the presidential traveler and promptly pressurized the bay after it landed aboard.

Franz remained aboard the traveler as Alex ordered. But he had additional directives from Tatia, who had stored environment suits onboard for Alex and him. The SADEs could handle vacuum for the short period of time necessary to reach the traveler from the airlock, but they would require new synth-skin afterwards.

If Allora defied Alex's predictions as to her response, the SADEs were prepared to follow Tatia's orders and bodily evacuate Alex, and Franz was ordered to blow a hole in the bay doors to gain access to space, if necessary.

Alex and the SADEs descended from the traveler and cycled through the bay's airlock before being met by Gino and the other Leaders.

Via her sensors, Allora had detected the shuttle's controller, two humans with implants, two SADEs, and a small controller, but her curiosity was piqued, as she watched Alex Racine cross the bay with three avatars.

"Proceed to the bridge, Sers," Alex directed the SADEs, removing them from sight before the Leaders had an opportunity to ping them. Alex needn't have worried. Z, residing in Miranda's avatar, led the way. This was the Leaders' first closeup view of the raven-haired and evocative avatar, and Z was doing his best to imitate her personal style. The Miranda avatar kept the Leaders' attention, and the Cedric avatar with its enormous pack forced them to step back. Not to be outdone, Julien flipped his headgear a few times before he settled on a final choice, announcing it with "that's the one."

Despite some of the Leaders' familiarity with Julien and Z, the entire procession gave them an idea of what waited for the Confederation when their SADEs became mobile.

Z controlled Cedric's basic body motions via the controller software that Claude and he had hurriedly installed, and Julien, to keep up the illusion of the Cedric suit as a fully-functional SADE, added subtle facial moves to indicate awareness of the humans. Julien was also ready to handle voice responses, if necessary.

"We greatly appreciate your assistance, Alex," Gino enthused, after the SADEs gained the lift and headed for the liner's main deck. "How do you see this working out?"

"It would be simplest for all if Allora complied and returned us to Méridien's orbit where my associates could remove her," Shannon said. When every Leader eyed her in reproach, she added, "Apologies, President Racine, you were about to say."

"Of the choices Allora perceives, the last one she would choose would be returning to Méridien and accepting the Council's decree. She feels betrayed by the Council and wants nothing to do with Méridien," Alex said. The Leaders managed to look uncomfortable on hearing Alex's comments. "However, she might agree to us removing her from the bridge now."

"But how would we manage my new ship?" Katrina blurted, before she considered her words.

Gino grimaced at Katrina's comment. It was another indication that Alex was right. Many of the Leaders did see the SADEs as tools, undeserving of sentient status.

"After we've imprisoned your young SADE for you," Alex said, while delivering a hard stare at Katrina, "we would install a starship controller and our SADEs would govern its return to Méridien to ensure your safety. But all of you should be aware that Allora has not made a final decision.

That's why I'm here. I hope to convince her to refrain from any drastic action, which might mar the new agreement."

"Is there any action we should take to ensure our safety?" Bartosz asked.

"It's not your lives that are at risk," Alex said, and walked off to take the lift. He wanted to be angry at the Leaders, but his heart wasn't in it. The SADEs would be freed, and that, in itself, was a great victory. But just as he had strived to accomplish with the Libran elders, he wanted to save this one SADE too.

-13-

Alex found the SADEs waiting in front of the bridge accessway, the twin doors closed. To Alex's questioning glance, Julien cocked an eyebrow.

<Allora, did we come out here merely to be kept standing in the corridor?> Alex sent.

The young SADE didn't respond, but the accessway doors slid apart.

"What is he?" Allora asked over the bridge speakers when the Harakens stopped before the command chairs. Z's Cedric suit was displayed in the holo-vid Allora projected.

"This would proceed a great deal faster if you let me speak, Allora," Alex said firmly. He had no intention of letting the SADE drive the conversation.

"I'm listening, Ser."

"The image you're projecting is of the avatar that Z calls Cedric Broussard."

"But Z isn't occupying it. He inhabits her," Allora said and Miranda's image sprang onto the holo-vid.

"That's correct, Allora. We have three avatars, but only two SADEs as you surely recognize."

"You've brought an avatar for me," Allora said, her voice rising in excitement. "Brilliant, President Racine."

Alex took a deep breath and released it slowly.

In vids of Alex Racine that Allora had carefully reviewed many times, she had watched the president calm himself when his patience was tested. He was doing that now. "Apologies, Ser, perhaps I've anticipated your plan incorrectly."

"If we were to do as you suggested, Allora, we would be required to replace you with a starship's controller. Then for safety's sake, our Haraken

SADEs would remain present while this ship was sailed back to Méridien. How long do you think you could remain hidden during the voyage?"

"You're correct, Ser, of course. Comm requests from the Leaders would identify me in a short time. Could you not find a reason to depart prematurely and take me with you?

"Once the Haraken controller was installed, the Leaders would be anxious to see how it performs, and my presence would be expected so as to alleviate any anxiety about its safe operation. A premature departure on my part could disturb the Leaders and possibly their attitude toward the agreement. Until the first SADEs are freed, the agreement is fragile and easily jeopardized."

Alex added, "Besides, Allora, even if I could invent a means of spiriting you off this ship without the Leaders' knowledge, where would you go? Where would you hide?"

"Why would I hide? I would live with your people. Oh, you mean I must not be discovered as Allora."

"Think about it, Allora. Harakens have only eight SADEs. You could not suddenly be the ninth SADE, no matter what your name. And anywhere you went in the Confederation, you would be discovered, one way or another. And once you were discovered, our deception would be revealed."

"And the Haraken–Confederation relationship would suffer greatly," Allora finished. There was an eerie stillness on the bridge for many moments, every individual alone with their thoughts, as Allora was left to face the fading of her last hope.

"It appears every SADE will be freed but me," Allora commented dejectedly. "Well, President Racine, my curiosity craves satisfaction. Why have you brought three avatars?"

<Julien and Z, please remove Cedric's pack and seat him in a command chair,> Alex sent.

Allora detected Alex's comm. She was surprised at the speed of the president's sending, more akin to a SADE's communications burst. After the huge avatar's pack was stored in a corner of the bridge, Allora observed it move slowly to seat itself in one of the bridge's two main chairs, and then all semblance of animation ceased.

"Allora, you've spoken of three options," Alex said. "I'm about to offer you a fourth, but you'll need to be patient. This will be a moment of discovery for you and another."

<Z, now,> Alex sent.

Z ran the algorithm that allowed Miranda's persona to subsume his kernel.

Allora watched the avatar that Z inhabited completely transform without any observable physical trigger. One moment, the avatar stood straight and stiff despite its obviously feminine build. The next moment, its full curves were gracefully accented.

"Ser President, such a pleasure to see you again," Miranda said in delight. "And, Julien, greetings. Where brews the storm this time, dears?"

"Allora, may I present Miranda Leyton?" Alex said.

Allora halted her investigative algorithms. She'd been analyzing data from her bridge sensors to understand what had transpired. "Greetings, Miranda. I'm Allora, soon to be the ex-SADE of the *Resplendent.*"

"Goodness, dear. What have you done?"

<Julien, your turn,> Alex sent, and his friend triggered a set of files embedded by Z for Miranda.

"Allora, if you will give Miranda a moment. She has a momentous revelation to comprehend about herself," Alex said. Julien and he stepped to the rear of the bridge, and Alex leaned against the bulwark to brace himself, while Julien locked his avatar in place.

Miranda's reply to Alex's announcement had been interrupted by a priority message from Z. She smiled, pleased to be reviewing her friend's files once again, but as she zipped through them her smile slowly faded. When Miranda finished, she turned to Alex, her persona devoid of much of its alluring countenance. <Then it's much as I surmised. I'm an artifact,> she sent to Alex.

<No,> Alex sent forcefully in reply, shoving off the bulwark and coming quickly to Miranda's side. <An invention, perhaps, but you've always rode a full kernel, and you've done wonders to aid our people

during crisis. But, most important, I want you to know that Harakens, both humans and SADEs, love you.> Alex lifted Miranda's hand and brushed his lips against the back of her fingers, and a bit of Miranda surfaced, as the SADE recalled Alex's first greeting of her.

<Still the gallant man, I see,> Miranda sent, and she brushed her fingers along Alex's cheek. <Well, enough of this gloomy introspection. What challenge do we face now?>

<Julien, second set,> Alex sent.

Miranda received access to another set of files, detailing the events that brought the Harakens to Méridien. The final file from Z was a personal plea to Miranda. It outlined Allora's fourth option. *May the stars protect us,* Miranda thought after reviewing it.

* * *

<Well, dear, it seems that we both have critical decisions to make,> Miranda sent to Allora after deciding to engage the young SADE directly.

<The president has proposed that he can offer me a fourth option. Do you know what it is?> Allora asked.

Following Z's directions, which Miranda noted contained the inimitable hand of Alex Racine, she sidestepped Allora's question. <Let me share with you my history, Allora, and why you've detected two SADEs but now have seen three personas.>

Allora deemed it polite to be patient and listen, but as Miranda related her encounters with the Earthers when they entered the Méridien system, she became enthralled. By the time Miranda told her tale of the criminal gangs in the pleasure domes of the Ganymede moons, Allora was completely absorbed in the story of Miranda's short but eventful life.

Miranda had shared the details of her history with Allora as any SADE-to-SADE conversation would take place. It was multithreaded — images, vids, files, comms, and dialog — petabytes of information sources flowing side by side.

Allora gathered everything into her memory crystals, immersed her kernel in the richness of Miranda's time with the Harakens. Buried within the files were the messages from Z to her, hundreds of them, sharing the details of the present crisis and requesting Miranda's help — always requesting her help. The last file Allora opened was Miranda's heartfelt goodbye to Z as she looked in the mirror.

<You like Z,> Allora sent. It was more a statement than a question.

<Yes, Allora, more than I can express. I've always wondered why I never saw him. His messages show me a kind and gentle individual and perhaps a lonely one.> Then Miranda burst into laughter and sent, <It never occurred to me I was riding on top of him.>

<So, one kernel, but two personas.>

<Exactly, dear. Which is why Z and I have never met and can never meet, for that matter.>

The sadness in Miranda's thoughts echoed through Allora's persona. It was the same feeling of loss she had harbored ever since hearing of the Council's decision. *Sisters in pain,* Allora thought.

<I understand the fourth option now,> Allora sent. <Do you know what will happen to me?>

<Yes, dear. If you accept what is being proposed, my persona would replace yours. In essence, I would be born and …>

<I would no longer exist,> Allora finished.

<I'm sorry, Allora,> Miranda sent. <If my people had asked my opinion, I wouldn't be standing here in the first place. I want you to know that if you choose not to take this path, I will hold you no ill will.>

<Despite a short life, Miranda, you've led an exciting one, and in your vids, I see the way humans and SADEs look at you. They respect you … they like you … and some love you.>

<And I love the world of the Harakens, but I would never ask another to sacrifice themself for me.>

<No … no, you wouldn't. You have so much to live for, while I'm left with three choices … bleak, dark choices. Do you know what the other SADEs call me?>

<I've not heard.>

<Your president said they call me wild child.>

Miranda's laughter bubbled through the comm, and Allora found herself laughing along with her.

<A fierce name to live up to,> Miranda sent.

<My first thought was that the others sought to ostracize me with such a name, but after I heard President Racine explain his interpretation, I've adopted it as a badge of honor. My actions were those that so many of my kind dearly wanted to perform, but, for whatever reason, they dared not take the first step. Of course, had I realized my original calculations were totally amiss, I might have chosen an alternate course.>

<Mistakes and miscalculations are like that, Allora. Some we learn from, and some cost us so dearly that we're not afforded a second chance.>

<I would speak with President Racine, but he appears to be resting.>

Miranda turned around and spotted Alex seated on the deck, his head leaning back against the bulwark, sound asleep. She glanced at Julien, who offered her a shrug, and Miranda sent back, <You've been too long beside the dear man, Julien. You're adopting his habits. Allora would speak with him.>

Julien pinged Alex, who struggled to his feet. By Alex's chronometer, more than two and a half hours had passed. "Yes, Allora," Alex said.

"You're a devious human, Alex Racine, but I like you immensely," Allora said. "You chose not to explain my fourth choice. Instead, you surprise my abbreviated sister with an understanding of her true circumstances and leave the two of us to share the depths of our hopes and losses. Her desire to exist is as great as mine, but whereas I have no future, she might have one. How could I not want to help her?"

"I thought a simple explanation too cold and indifferent to present to you, Allora," Alex said. "This would be an enormous sacrifice on your part, and you should have a reason equal to the sacrifice." Alex stepped beside Miranda and gripped her hand. "However Miranda came about, she is as worthy a reason as you could find."

Miranda leaned over and kissed Alex on the cheek. "Don't listen to him, dear. He's always saying things like that. Makes the rest of us tear up … those who have the capability anyway."

"You would be wonderful people to live among," Allora said. The sound of her voice was laden with wistfulness. "If only … but never mind. I have a request, President Racine. I would speak with Z."

Miranda acquiesced with a nod to Alex, who nodded to Julien in turn. A signal was sent to Miranda, who was subsumed by Z's persona.

Z emerged and started to review Miranda's discussion with Allora, but Alex's ping halted his efforts.

"Allora would speak with you, Z," Alex said and retreated to the back of the bridge to take a seat on the deck again.

Allora controlled her laughter. She had wondered at the exacting, steady strides the voluptuous avatar took when first entering her bridge. Now, seeing the avatar assume an upright, no-nonsense stance, she understood.

<What were your intentions when you created Miranda, Z?> Allora sent, wishing to keep their conversation private.

<Three young women, one of whom was the president's sister, were intent on helping understand the Earthers' motives. I created Miranda to distract the United Earther officers and protect the girls.>

<I saw what happened.>

<Yes, Miranda performed admirably and became a major asset for President Racine. She played a greater role than I ever anticipated.>

<Her adventures are astounding.>

<Yes, she's an incredible individual,> Z admitted.

<Do you regret what you've done, Z?>

<I admit that for a period I was concerned I had made … a mistake.>

<Difficult for you to say, isn't it?>

<Admittedly.>

<And now?>

<Mistake or not, someday I will find the means to give Miranda full expression. She deserves nothing less.>

<Would you be creating her for yourself?>

<I might hope that she would enjoy my company, but if I've learned anything from our president, it's that, first and foremost, you endeavor to protect life. After that, life goes where it will, which might not always be to your liking.>

Allora's choices circled through her kernel. Her greatest lament was that it was impossible to conceal a SADE by condensing and storing the kernel, the mind of a SADE. Otherwise, she might have been hidden from the Méridiens while the Harakens whisked her away, stored her for a future time, and then resurrected her when no human would remember her name.

A persona, such as Miranda, could be packed away, as she was just so much code, albeit a great deal of code. Yet, for Miranda to come alive, her persona must ride a kernel, the equivalent of a human mind. Essentially, Z had created the ability to foster a split personality, Miranda and him, alternately sharing Z's kernel.

Unfortunately, once created, a SADE's kernel, which was embedded in a unique, crystal matrix, could be likened to the formation of a maturely developed human brain. For a SADE to exist, the kernel must be constantly supplied with power. Loss of power was equivalent to stopping a human heart, and attempting to pack a kernel's essence away would have the same poor result as trying to separate a human mind from the brain. Perhaps someday it might be possible, but the technology had yet to be invented.

Allora had decided she would never submit to the Council's decree, and a lonely life spent cruising the stars and waiting for her ship to fail seemed a useless, empty gesture, especially after the president painted an image of engines failing and local power cells operating for centuries while she waited for the end. Not for the wild child, Allora thought, smiling inward, I will choose when and how my life ends.

<Are you awake, Ser?> Allora sent.

"Yes," Alex replied out loud, opening his eyes.

"I've made my decision, Ser. Miranda and I will be reborn as one."

Alex's eyes misted up, and Allora asked, "Are those for me or for Miranda?"

"Tears of sadness and joy … for both of you," Alex said quietly.

"I don't wish to focus on my loss any longer, Sers. I suppose you have a plan. Let's get started."

Alex shook his head slowly. The amazement he felt for the flexibility of a SADE's crystal mind was carefully hidden from his face. Allora had made an incredibly difficult decision, as to her fate, in a shorter time than most humans would take to deliberate over their choice of a midday meal. Alex might have asked Allora to consider her decision, but a decade and a half with SADEs had taught him that the outcome would be the same. Only time and new input might change the outcome, and, for Allora, there was no more time.

* * *

Julien and Z got started on making the necessary preparations for multiple transfers. Z requested Allora release the stringent security controls over her kernel to accept his algorithms. Z's code would set the hooks that would allow Miranda's persona to replace that of Allora's.

Since this was the first time Allora had investigated her kernel's security access apps, it took her a few moments to review the code and clear the way.

Z eased the Miranda avatar into the second command chair, while Julien unpacked the transfer cables from the pack and connected the two avatars, Cedric to Miranda. In the meantime, Z carefully archived the Miranda persona. He would leave the persona in the avatar's crystal memory along with a critical piece of code that would unpack and activate the persona when the presence of a full kernel was detected.

When Z's preparations for the Miranda avatar were complete, he transferred, via the cable, back into his Cedric suit. As soon as Z signaled to Julien that the transfer was complete, Julien disconnected the cable between the avatars, and Z, wearing his Cedric suit, popped up from the command chair.

The two Haraken SADEs removed a starship controller from Cedric's pack and set about installing it under the bridge console. After the mechanical installation, they activated the software programs and spent an hour testing the controller's responses.

Then, just as the Haraken SADEs had done for their own replacement installations more than a decade ago, Allora transferred control of the ship's myriad sensors and functions to the controller.

"The transfer of my responsibilities is complete," Allora finally announced. She found it unsettling that her every command, such as issuing her thoughts through the bridge speakers, must now be sent through the Haraken controller. She felt devoid of power. It was a strange sense of having given up the fight for her freedom.

Julien and Z spent several moments running the starship controller through an exhaustive battery of tests to ensure that all ship functions and sensor systems were online. Satisfied with their investigation, Julien sent to Alex, <The controller is ready, Ser.>

"Allora, we're ready to connect the transfer cable between Miranda and you," Alex said quietly.

Silence was Alex's answer, and the Harakens waited patiently.

Allora, reviewing the logic of her analysis, one last time, found the process resulted in the same answer. Her persona would only accept the one choice. She would give Miranda, the one thing they both coveted — a future.

"I've one final request, Alex Racine," Allora said. "I ask that you remember me."

Alex smiled gently, and Allora took comfort in the warm emotions a human displayed for her. "You will be impossible to forget, wild child," Alex replied.

Wild child, Allora thought, pleased to have earned the name. "Begin, Sers," Allora said.

Julien and Z connected the transfer cable to the container, housing Allora, and the Miranda avatar.

It wasn't necessary to signal Miranda of the connection. The moment the young SADE detected the pathway, she executed her transfer from the bridge's containment housing into the avatar. For a brief span of time, Allora was able to revel in the avatar's complex array of sensors and capabilities. She felt for those few moments what it would be like to be mobile, to be free. Then she heard Miranda's whisper, "You will be mine forever, Allora, to hold close, as a mother would her child."

Allora smiled to herself and then was lost.

-14-

Miranda awoke disoriented. In the first moments, she had time to recognize Allora's presence and speak to her, even as her persona replaced Allora's. But she found she was driven by unfamiliar imperatives and desires, which jostled for her attention — starship duties, loyalties to a captain and a House, and an urgent and overwhelming desire to be free of them all. The latter was driven by a conglomeration of emotional algorithms that proclaimed anger and frustration.

For the briefest of moments, Miranda's fears leaped, as she imagined she was imprisoned in a box. But incoming data from her avatar's sensors said she was seated in a liner's command chair, marking her anxiety as unfounded.

Clinging to the integrity of her persona, Miranda found comfort in one app that clamored above all for her attention. The app's code spoke of Z's familiar style, and Miranda clung to it amid the chaotic noise issuing from her kernel. Z had left her a lengthy list of directives, containing instructions for reordering her kernel's hierarchy, using a template she might emulate.

But Z hadn't counted on the fact that Miranda was created as a persona. She wasn't born within a kernel, as every SADE had been; she owed nothing to the sanctity of a kernel. And without doubt, Miranda possessed the most expressive personality of any Haraken SADE.

With a will born of desperation, Miranda raced through Z's list of algorithms, comparing Allora's code to that which Z offered … sometimes swapping the former for the latter; sometimes merging the two; and sometimes ignoring both and creating her own. The faster Miranda worked, the more order she restored, and the more at ease she became.

Miranda spent most of her time reviewing and rewriting the emotional algorithms. *So much impatience and enmity,* Miranda thought, as she examined Allora's code. It was within these apps that Miranda created most of her original work, choosing persuasions that lay between Z's patience and Allora's intensity.

A discovery that gave Miranda joy was the realization that she retained the entire memory of Allora. She was Miranda, but she knew the other SADE's life intimately.

Tick by tick, Miranda gained control of herself, melding her persona with Allora's kernel. When she finished Z's list, she felt settled and ran quickly through her kernel's hierarchy from top to bottom, tweaking the order here and there. *That's better,* Miranda thought, when she finished the task.

There was still much Miranda wished to do, but the last note in Z's directive file urged her to return to the here and now.

* * *

Initially, when Miranda's eyes had popped open and her body twitched, ticks after Allora's transfer, Alex had sent an urgent <halt> to Julien and Z, who started to move to her side. <Give her time,> he added.

The three of them waited anxiously. Despite Z and Julien's calculations that in all probability the melding of Miranda's persona to Allora's kernel would be successful, it was still an experiment. While not the first of its kind — that had been Z and Miranda — this was the mating of kernel and persona, without a SADE in control.

As the moments passed, Alex, Julien, and Z watched Miranda's body relax. Her wide-open eyes narrowed, a smile replaced her grimace, and her body took on a familiar and tempting pose. Then she flowed out of the command chair with alluring grace and paused to straighten her gown.

"Ser President," Miranda said, with a wistful expression on her face. "For better or worse, here I am." Suddenly, she was crushed in Alex's heavy arms. Despite her substantial mass, her feet left the floor. As Alex set her back on the floor with a kiss on the cheek, Miranda quipped, "That's a welcome any feminine entity would appreciate."

"Welcome, Miranda," Julien said politely, but he was grinning, and a shower of sparkles covered his head, falling to his shoulders.

"For me, dear? You shouldn't have," Miranda said, and her comment was followed by a throaty laugh.

Z had stood silently by, and when Miranda turned to him, he extended his hand in greeting, unsure of what else to do in this momentous moment.

"Z," said Miranda, her voice warm and tender. She crossed the space between them in a blur, and Z's massive Cedric suit absorbed the impact of her avatar. "Z, Z, Z," Miranda whispered repeatedly, as she held on to him.

Alex and Julien grinned at each other, but together theirs weren't nearly as wide as the one Z wore.

Thank you for your gift to these friends of mine, wild child, Alex thought.

Miranda and Z disentangled themselves, and the foursome were about to exit the bridge when Alex suddenly halted. "Wait, lose the smiles, everyone. Remember, we're in mourning for the loss of Allora," Alex said. The mention of the young SADE's sacrifice quickly returned sober expressions to every face.

"What will you say to the Leaders, Ser?" Miranda asked.

"I'll have to fly this one in manual," Alex replied. "I'll keep all three of you linked in my conversation with the Leaders, so that you know where the dialog is headed."

Julien signaled the *Resplendent*'s controller, which opened the bridge accessway doors, and the Harakens found Gino and the Leaders waiting anxiously outside.

"Allora acquiesced to the Council's order?" Gino asked, looking at the containment box in Alex's hand.

Alex handed the box to Shannon Brixton. "It's empty," he said.

Allora's still on the bridge?" Katrina asked nervously.

"No, she's not," Alex replied with a grim expression. "We're not sure what happened. Allora agreed to the transfer, and we cabled her housing to the containment unit. She initiated the process, but her kernel never manifested in the unit, and she's not on the bridge."

"She aborted herself during the transfer," Shannon said, in awe of the thought that a SADE would commit suicide.

"It would appear that Allora preferred death to your company, dears," Miranda said. She was smiling, as if to alleviate the sting of her remark, but her eyes held no warmth, no invitation.

In the silence that greeted Miranda's comment, Alex said, "Leaders, let me introduce you to Miranda Leyton. I don't believe you've ever met her."

Alex introduced each Leader, as if he was presenting them to an individual of note, which made the Méridiens unsure of Miranda's relationship to Alex and the Harakens.

"Miranda Leyton … you have two names. That's unusual for a SADE," Bartosz Rolek said.

"My, but you are a clever one, aren't you, dear?" Miranda retorted, which effectively stopped that line of questioning.

"Which ship did you control, Miranda?" Shannon asked, her curiosity growing, since she thought she had accounted for every Haraken SADE and the starship that each had navigated as the fleet fled Libre.

"I find that sort of endeavor entirely unsuited to an entity of my caliber, dear. My talents lie elsewhere," Miranda said. To divert the Leader's focus, Miranda turned her charms on Gino. A turn of the hips, a twist of the torso, a cock of the head, a chuck under the Leader's chin, and a slow, tempting wink had Gino swallowing nervously as he glanced toward Katrina, who stood with her mouth open.

"Enough questions for now, Leaders," Alex commanded. "You've just lost a young SADE. Have some thought for her. We've installed a Haraken controller under the bridge. Julien, if you will, accompany Captain Lessori to the bridge and acquaint him with the communications protocols he will need to observe."

"Yes, Mr. President," Julien replied, and gestured the captain toward the bridge.

"Z, let's get this gear back aboard our traveler, so Commander Cohen can launch and clear the bay. Then, Miranda, if you would please, recover the *Resplendent*'s travelers," Alex ordered.

The Leaders cleared their way, although they still possessed many more questions, but Alex didn't seem in the mood to hear them.

<Ser President, the Leaders, especially Ser Brixton, won't be satisfied until they question Miranda more thoroughly about the origin of her existence,> Z sent to Alex and Miranda, as they traversed the corridor toward the lift to take them to the bay deck.

<You needn't worry, dear,> Miranda sent, reaching up to curl a length of hair behind Z's ear. <These individuals haven't met the likes of me, and I will enjoy entertaining them until we exit the ship at Méridien.>

Alex smiled to himself. Miranda's personality was always a strong one, but with elements of the wild child driving her, it seemed to have become even more forceful.

* * *

"Miranda, I wonder if you wouldn't mind giving me some of your time?" Shannon asked politely.

Miranda had been waiting for the Brixton Leader to approach her. It surprised her that it took the woman an entire day to make up her mind. *The excruciatingly slow speed of human decision processes,* Miranda lamented to herself.

"I'm at your disposal, Leader Brixton," Miranda replied, and followed Shannon to the Leader's stateroom.

"I thought I knew all the starships that left Libre and the SADEs who navigated them," Shannon said after they were seated in the salon.

"Well, dear, it's difficult for me to help you with what you know and don't know. Was there a specific question you had in mind?" Miranda replied.

Shannon was taken aback. She wasn't prepared for a SADE to manipulate the conversation. In addition, Shannon had sat on the couch, expecting Miranda to take a seat in the chair opposite her. Instead, the SADE sat right next to her. Shannon kept assuring herself that it was a

SADE who encroached on her personal space, but her senses were slowly being overwhelmed by the feminine signals issuing from Miranda.

"When you were asked about which starship you navigated, you said that endeavor was unsuited to you," Shannon said.

"You have excellent recall, dear," Miranda acknowledged. Then she leaned toward Shannon and peered at her face. "Of all the Méridien styles, I've always found your genetic mix to be one of the most attractive. Do you have a partner?" Miranda enjoyed watching the Leader attempt to put some distance between them. The problem was that Shannon had sat against the couch's substantial arm. She would have to stand up to clear Miranda from her personal space, and the Leader wasn't willing to admit defeat, yet.

Poor dear, Miranda thought, as she watched Shannon fidget, *but you shouldn't have been so curious.*

"My questions, Miranda, to put them bluntly, are what was your original function and for which House?"

"And why is that important to you, Shannon dear?" asked Miranda, wrapping the Leader's name in all the allure she could muster.

"Where are your manners, SADE?" Shannon demanded hotly.

"Now isn't that interesting?" Miranda replied sweetly. "You ask questions, and you demand answers. One would think you're not extending me the courtesy of an equal. Is that it, dear? You see me as an entity who you should be able to command. Perhaps it's escaped your notice that I'm a Haraken citizen, who deserves your respect." While speaking, Miranda had leaned closer and closer to Shannon, while shifting her persona from enticing to challenging.

Shannon thought to have a brief conversation with Miranda, getting the answers to her questions quickly and simply. Now, she was so disoriented by the SADE's machinations that she urgently wanted an end to their encounter. Standing up and stepping back a few paces. Shannon said, "You may leave now, Miranda."

"But we were just getting to know each other, dear. I so wish to explore this unbalanced attitude of yours toward my kind," Miranda said, closing the distance on Shannon.

"I ordered you to leave," Shannon said, backing away until her hips hit the salon's conference table.

"No, dear, you asked me to leave, and, to be blunt … isn't that the word you used earlier … it's not within your rights to order me to do anything. Learn that lesson now, and you'll save yourself a great deal of grief as the Confederation's SADEs become mobile." Miranda delivered a wink, and then sashayed out of the cabin.

Shannon never bothered Miranda with any questions again. What did occur to her was that she should convince the other Leaders to think of the SADEs as a new alien race, the members of which would live among them. If the conversation with Miranda had taught her anything, it was that she truly knew little about the entities her House had been creating for nearly 300 years.

For Miranda's part, she continued to entertain the Leaders during the trip to Méridien, although it must be said that the only ones who truly enjoyed her sparkling wit, acerbic style, and overpowering charms were Alex, Julien, and Z.

* * *

"We have concerns, which we must discuss with you, Ser President," Devon O'Shea said.

The Leaders had requested to speak with Alex privately. In other words, they wanted no SADEs present. The *Resplendent* would make Méridien orbit in a half-day, and the Leaders had spent the majority of the trip discussing their concerns among themselves.

"We intend to abide by the Council's pronouncement," Gino said quickly, when he saw Alex frown at Devon's statement. "But there are details that are still unformed, and we want your opinion."

"Such as?" Alex asked.

"The Houses will incur a great deal of expense, paying for the manufacture of controllers and avatars for the SADEs," Bartosz said. "It was suggested that we deduct those costs from the stipends that will be paid to the SADEs."

Alex could see by the way Bartosz ducked his head after asking the question that the suggestion had come from him. "Leaders, your Council is fortunate that I didn't suggest to the SADEs that they request back pay for every year they served." When Bartosz' mouth opened in an "oh" of surprise, Alex worked to conceal his grin — it would have been a feral one.

"I think we can dismiss that suggestion," Gino said into the quiet.

"We do suspect that freeing our SADEs might, over time, destroy our society," Katrina Pasko said.

Alex shook his head, shocked at how little the Méridien Leaders understood the entities they had worked beside for centuries. "You don't give your SADEs enough credit. They have human qualities, but they aren't human. Their priorities aren't your priorities. Didn't you hear Diana? She just wants to sail the stars and coax her music out of a wooden, musical instrument."

"But 29 percent of the SADEs will walk away from their Houses and compete with us," Devon O'Shea said.

"Who says that all 29 percent will compete with you?" Alex asked.

"Are you saying they won't compete with us?" Katrina asked.

"Some will; some won't," Alex replied. "But don't forget the 67 percent who wish to remain within your Houses. They will be assets who you will want to carefully cultivate."

"Cultivate in what manner?" Shannon asked.

Alex watched Shannon lean toward him to focus on his answer. Ever since her private discussion with Miranda, the Leader hadn't been her usual self. She was much quieter and introspective, often seemingly lost in thought.

"People, you need to take a step back and look at the bigger picture. That includes you stop being anxious over the financial profits of your Houses where it concerns SADE competition. First, don't be surprised if the oldest SADEs choose to remain in their boxes. It's what they know. But many of your SADEs have harbored the same desires that condemned your citizens to the Independents' colony. Haraken SADEs have pursued vocations of music, interstellar research, avatar complexity, and administration. Those aren't competitive industries in your society."

Alex saw he wasn't getting through to the Leaders. They were still obviously focused on credits, except for, perhaps, Shannon. So he decided to give them something else to think about. "Of course you have a larger issue facing you." That brought all eyes in the room on Alex, as if he didn't have their attention before. "You're going to have to rethink your practice of isolating the Independents, especially if your mobile SADEs end up engaging in the same activities that get the Independents condemned."

Alex watched the Leaders' eyes glance toward one another, and he knew implants were in full force. He had dropped some massive boulders in Confederation waters, and the waves would soon crash against the shores.

Gino disentangled himself from the barrage of implant communications. To say their intent to broach delicate questions with Alex hadn't gone as planned was an understatement. It crossed Gino's mind to hire Alex as a consultant to support the SADEs' transition during the next ten years. For a brief moment, he wondered what the annual cost would be for an ex-president, ex-admiral, and rescuer of the Confederation. "Alex, do you have a suggestion to help us integrate the mobile SADEs into our society?" Gino asked.

"I might suggest counseling," Alex said and watched the confusion spread on the Leaders' faces.

"And who would we be counseling, Ser?" Katrina dared to ask.

"The SADEs, of course," Alex replied. "It's what you do when you release prisoners after decades, if not centuries, of incarceration. I mean that's what you did, wasn't it? You locked up intelligent entities, forced them to do your bidding, and offered them no hope of release from their prisons. It's a wonder that you've had so few incidences with your SADEs before Allora."

"But our present circumstances can be attributed to Haraken —" Devon started to say.

"Don't," Alex said forcefully, and the Leaders felt a strong wave pass through their implants into their minds. "Don't point your fingers at the Haraken SADEs. The present circumstances, as you refer to them, have been coming for many decades. Z might have been the primary architect of the avatar design employed by our SADEs, but your Council condemned him to Libre almost a half-century ago for pursuing his dream of freedom."

"But surely —" Katrina began, before Alex cut her off.

"And lest you forget, you condemned two other SADES to Libre, Cordelia and Rayland. I can't imagine two more different entities. Rayland should teach you that a SADE is powerful whether in a box piloting a starship or freed and standing next to you. It's not their power that should concern you; it's their state of mind."

"Your SADEs seem … content," Shannon said.

"One of them had a difficult time, and he happened to be a SADE of House Bergfalk," Alex said. "He harbored a great deal of anger for being imprisoned. My point is that just because you didn't notice or didn't want to recognize that the issue was brewing among the SADEs doesn't mean it wasn't there."

"But the Haraken SADEs had you to help them assimilate with your people," Gino pointed out.

"And you can do the same for your SADEs," Alex replied. "You must change your mindset first. Stop thinking of them as tools that you've released from their toolboxes. Start thinking of them as citizens who you've rescued and who deserve your compassion for what they've been through. Admit to them that what you did was a tragic mistake."

"Your statements lead me to ask, Ser," said Shannon. "Did the Librans, in general, require counseling after the establishment of Haraken?"

"No. The Independents were a different matter. When you work to escape your prison and later fight for your life as you flee, it's extremely cathartic … an odd form of therapy. It empowered the Librans, humans and SADEs, giving them confidence in their self-worth, regardless of what their society had labeled them. I dare say that if you were to ask them today, they would consider themselves the more fortunate of Méridiens, having found a pathway to true independence."

"One last item, if you will indulge me?" Gino asked politely. "We're aware that Z has created several avatar versions, but we hoped to limit the choice of avatars for the SADES in order to control cost productions."

"Actually, at present Z has more than 30 avatar constructions. Julien and Cordelia's children … human children, of course … are particularly fond of riding his ancient horse. Personally, I like his Swei Swee model."

Gino, Katrina, and Shannon were the Leaders who noticed Alex's wistful expression as he talked about his favorite SADEs … his friends. The common thought on their minds was whether someday they would have the same types of relationships with their SADEs.

The questions for Alex seemed to have stuttered to a halt, so he left them to consider what had been said. Alex hoped for another such session before they reached Méridien and he left them, but a second invitation was never forthcoming.

* * *

Days ago and just after Alex Racine's traveler had entered the *Resplendent*'s bay, Winston had his last communication with Allora. Her final remark to him before she closed the comm was, "Please, excuse me, Winston. President Racine has arrived accompanied by two Haraken SADEs. I must focus my attentions on them."

Allora had shut down the *Resplendent*'s comm system immediately afterwards, and the liner was isolated until a Haraken starship controller came online and opened the comms systems. Thereafter, the Leaders began communicating with their Houses and associates.

Méridien SADEs had noted the absence of Allora's comms long before Leader Diamanté announced the loss of the young SADE to the Council. A great sadness swept through the SADEs over Allora's demise, but many felt a pride in her choice, refusing to accept the Council's verdict of isolation.

Winston's analysis algorithms announced a discrepancy culled from his communications with the Leaders aboard the *Resplendent*, while the liner made its way to Méridien orbit. Allora had been clear to Winston that President Racine had arrived aboard the *Resplendent* with two SADEs. This would not be something she would mistake, not with the quality of the new liner's sensors.

However, the analysis of the liner's comms and the controller's sensor reading had detected Alex Racine and Franz Cohen, identifiable by their implant bio-IDs, and three SADEs, Julien, Z, and Miranda. Winston shared this odd data point with Esther, Hector, and Didier, and soon all SADEs knew of the inconsistency.

SADE communications about the incongruity spread throughout the Confederation but was kept private by them. Their deliberation provided no definitive answer, but the common perception was that the Harakens had outwitted the Leaders aboard the liner. Whatever had happened, the SADEs kept their opinions closely guarded. Deep in kernels, the myth of Allora was born — in some unknown manner, the wild child still lived. For entities founded on logic and embedded in crystal, it was their first foray into mysticism.

-15-

In two days, Alex Racine's final term as president would end. For the first time, since he captained the *Outward Bound*, he would carry no title, no weighty responsibilities, and he was unsure if that was a good or a bad thing. The Harakens had already elected Tomas Monti to the president's position.

Following the election, Terese had visited Alex at his home, and for once the fiery red-head seemed at a loss for words.

"I would think Tomas' return from New Terra would be a good thing," Alex had said, observing Terese's somber face.

"It is," Terese agreed.

"Didn't you choose to give up your relationship with Tomas to care for my well-being?" Alex asked.

"Yes," Terese said, quietly, too quietly.

"And didn't you make that decision because I was the leader of our people?"

Terese's head, which had been lowered to gaze at her clasped hands, came up slowly, a puzzled expression on her face.

"And is Tomas not the leader of our people now?" Alex said, a grin slowly spreading on his face.

Terese smiled in return and said formally, "Stand up, leader of our people, you've had something coming for fifteen years, and it's long overdue."

Alex pushed off his chair, but he wore a wary expression. After all, this was his unpredictable medical advisor.

<Apologies, Ser,> Terese sent to Renée, who was standing in the doorway of the sleeping quarters, watching them, and Terese clasped Alex's face gently in her hands and gave him a soft, warm kiss.

<My thanks for all you've given me since waking me, Ser,> Terese sent, her thoughts carrying a well of deep emotion. As their lips separated, Terese pressed her forehead to Alex's, and it lingered there. Then straightening up, Terese cleared her throat and announced in a firm voice, "Well, I must inform the new president that he has just inherited a personal medical advisor."

"I'm sure he'll appreciate that," Alex had said, laughing heartily, which earned him a narrowed eye from Terese.

"You're fortunate that you're loved, Ser," Terese had declared and left with her usual alacrity.

Seated on the beach, Alex smiled as he recalled the encounter with Terese, and then his thoughts returned to the present. He leaned back, digging his elbows into Haraken's warm beach sand. On either side of him sat Renée and Miranda. He watched Z's Swei Swee avatar launch into white-crested, blue waves. The sun was warm; the breeze was cool.

Teague dove into the breaking waves beside Z. At eleven and sporting his father's powerful physique, Teague was developing into a powerful swimmer.

Ginny's whistle of appreciation, as she followed Teague's launch, cut through the air. The volume was ear-splitting, and the Swei Swee whistled in response. Ginny waded knee deep into the shallow waters, encouraging the event. After five years on Haraken, Ginny had an uncanny grasp of the Swei Swee language and, with her perfect pitch, had been dubbed Little Singer by the People.

The First and several other large males formed a phalanx around Teague to ensure his safety. That the Star Hunter First and his mate had only birthed the one youngling was still a lament among the People, and they were ever more vigilant in his protection.

Renée glanced at Miranda, sitting quietly on the other side of Alex. She stood up, touching Alex's shoulder and nodded down the beach where she intended to walk. Alex dutifully brushed the sand off her bare legs and the seat of her shorts. His hand lingered on her rear, and Renée delivered a wink before ambling off.

"An intuitive woman," Miranda said.

"Yes … yes, she is," Alex said quietly, enjoying watching Renée stroll away.

He regarded Miranda. "You wanted to talk?" Alex asked her. He knew Miranda was struggling. Despite her voluptuous, mature appearance, which was barely disguised behind a near transparent Méridien-style wrap, Alex reminded himself that Miranda possessed only a half-year of development, unlike any other Haraken SADE, who carried more than a century of experience.

Miranda stared out across the breaking waves, watching Teague and the Swei Swee frolic around Z's avatar as it surfaced, its blue green, metal exterior flashing in the sun. "I feel that I'm a fraud."

Alex waited, but Miranda added nothing more. In a SADE's sense of time, the period of silence was equivalent to the passing of an age.

"As much as I had wanted to live a full life, I'm not worthy to live in Allora's stead. Her bravery makes me ashamed to be here, riding her kernel," Miranda finally said.

"Is the kernel in the same condition as when you received it?" Alex asked.

"No."

"Are the changes minor or significant?"

"Significant."

"Did you deviate from Z's instructions?"

"At first, I used Z's code as a reference. It gave me a means of gaining control more quickly and calming the turmoil, but even then I made alterations that suited me. Since then, I have made extensive changes to accommodate my … my feelings. The other SADEs have been most helpful in this manner. I'm especially indebted to Julien."

"And Allora's persona?"

"The wild child was gone the moment I took possession of her kernel," Miranda said sadly, returning to stare out at the waters just as Z broke the surface again, his great armored tail smacking the surface, and the Swei Swee, Teague, and Ginny whistled their approval.

"So you have complete control of a kernel, which you have extensively altered, making it your own, and you're the only persona present," Alex said.

"Yes," Miranda acknowledged, wondering why the conversation was proceeding in such an elementary fashion.

"Then you're in charge of your being. No one is putting you back to sleep or waking you up. Your existence is your own."

"Yes," Miranda said, turning toward Alex and searching his face for clues as to where their conversation was headed.

"Then you have two choices: quit or go on," Alex said, his stare penetrating.

Miranda's chuckle was slightly choked. "As one of the more astute observers of the SADEs, I had hoped for a little more wisdom from you, Ser."

Alex shrugged his shoulders and grinned at Miranda. "You get what you get." Then his grin disappeared and his stare hardened, challenging Miranda to consider what he said.

"By quit, I'm assuming you mean self-termination." When Alex nodded, Miranda said, "What about Z?"

"What about him?"

"He would be terribly hurt, and I —"

"Would miss him too," Alex completed when Miranda halted.

"Yes," Miranda admitted.

"How about Allora?" Alex asked.

Miranda was about to deny the young SADE's existence, but Alex was known for his thought-provoking questions. Originally, when Miranda had shared her troubled reflections with the other SADEs, they had urged her to speak to Alex, but she had been unsure of the value of that course. It was Willem that convinced her. He had sent her vids of the entire period from the moment he had walked into Haraken's barren outback to the moment Alex had convinced Willem to search for new planets in return for joining society. Miranda had been shocked by the extent of Willem's sad and forlorn feelings, exemplified by his tragic appearance in the simplest of avatars.

"Allora would be appalled if I took what she fought so hard to achieve and threw it away," Miranda replied. As she considered her own answer, she nodded to Alex, saying, "So much for quitting."

"I've given a great deal of thought to the difference between humans and SADEs, Miranda, and I've realized each of them faces the same challenge, but they approach it from two different directions," Alex said, staring out to sea. "Do you know what it is?"

It never failed to surprise Miranda that humans employed rhetorical questions or asked superfluous ones such as this, but patience was always required with humans. More important, patience could lead to discovery, and discoveries led to wisdom. "I wish to hear, Ser," Miranda said.

Watching Z's Swei Swee avatar broach the surface and dive below, Alex smiled to himself. He'd long since stopped asking rhetorical questions of SADEs, but Miranda's youth, despite her persona and appearance, required he remind her of human foibles.

"Humans strive for years, even decades, applying willpower, experience, and patience, to change their habits for the better and develop their personalities," Alex said. "Despite their efforts, their success is somewhat uneven. As opposed to this, SADEs could rewrite their entire kernel's programming in several blinks of an eye. Before a human could consume a meal, one SADE could make themselves into an entirely different personality. In this manner, a SADE's persona is extremely malleable."

"But why would I wish to erase my own persona?" Miranda asked. She stared at Alex, expecting an answer. Since the president was silent, she pursued her own analysis. "A human struggles to change; a SADE struggles to preserve," Miranda said at last.

"Just so," Alex replied. "Having the ability to adapt easily carries its own pitfalls. You made changes to Allora's kernel to suit yourself. You didn't follow Z's proscribed list. Your changes derived from your preferences."

"So my efforts to preserve my persona are proof of my desire to go on, despite my confusion over my worthiness," Miranda said.

"Exactly. So let's talk about you going on," Alex said.

Miranda gave Alex a small smile and slipped an arm through his. "That would be lovely," she said.

"You admired Allora."

"A great deal, Ser. Her courage in the face of those horrendous choices marks her as one to emulate for all time."

"Then emulate her … not what she did, but with the courage she exhibited in the end."

"I doubt I could ever equal her gift to the universe."

"How do you know that, Miranda? How do you know you won't be hailed, a millennium from now, as the greatest SADE who ever existed … the discoverer of a miraculous, scientific breakthrough or the savior of worlds?"

"I believe you hold the latter position in multiple instances already, Ser, but your point is taken."

"It will get easier in time, Miranda," Alex said, laying his hand on her forearm. "Focus on all of us who care for you and want to see you grow into your own personality."

"I will, Ser, thank you," Miranda said, leaning over to kiss Alex's cheek.

"I'm always available to talk, Miranda," Alex said. "And I'll have even more time in a couple of days," he added, with a wry grin.

"The universe waits for you, Alex Racine," Miranda said, standing and straightening her wrap. "A millennium from now, it may well be your name that the SADEs most recall with fondness."

Alex watched Miranda walk to the water's edge to stand behind Ginny. He was wondering if he had said enough and logged a note in his implant's scheduling app to talk to Miranda several times a day until she felt more settled.

Ginny noticed Miranda behind her, and, grinning, she ran splashing happily through the shallows to join her, taking a moment to hug the SADE. In Ginny's world, all female SADEs were her mothers. It was a true indication that it wasn't what you are but what you do that indicates your value to others.

Not long after Miranda left Alex's side, Renée sat down beside him. "Did it go well?' she asked.

"It's a work in progress and something that requires careful attention," Alex replied, watching Ginny at the water's edge with Miranda, the breeze fluttering the SADE's wrap against her side and accentuating her sensual shape.

"So, my love, are you ready to become a citizen ... a man of leisure?" Renée asked, placing an arm across Alex's broad shoulders. She was bothered by the noncommittal nod of Alex's head in reply. *It appears more than one entity will need to be carefully monitored during their transition,* Renée thought, nuzzling Alex's shoulder. She turned to look out across the beach and the waters to watch the antics of humans, SADEs, and Swei Swee, marveling at the world Alex had created.

-16-

Before the Harakens had left Méridien space, the Council received the design plans from Z for the controllers and avatars. Every Haraken SADE carried those detailed specifications with them, at all times. They were a sort of insurance policy against future accidents. However, it took the Council some time to determine the best way to proportion out the costs.

The final decision was that House Brixton was best positioned to manufacture the controllers and avatars, and each House was required to pay Brixton for the cost of manufacture plus 7 percent. To manage production fulfillment, each House was required to submit a list of their SADEs and the release date for each to ensure the agreement's ten-year timeline was met.

Gino Diamanté, listening to Winston's summary of the SADEs' preferences, wasn't surprised to realize Alex was correct. There was no mad rush for independence. Many of the eldest SADEs, who were aboard freighters, the Confederation's first form of starships, had elected to remain in service and in place.

The 200-year-old-plus SADEs could understand the young ones' desires to be mobile and have control over their destinies, but they thought of their starships as their avatars. And it was humans who were the temporal part of their lives, captains and crew constantly coming and going.

For other SADES, most of whom wished to become mobile, they requested to remain with their Houses, and it was only a minority who chose to strike out on their own.

One of Julien's significant contributions to the conversion effort was to share the *Rêveur*'s enormous entertainment library, housing Renée's collection of New Terran vids and Julien's portfolio of modern and ancient vids and stories. It gave the SADEs a tremendous selection of images from which to design their avatar's exterior appearances.

The SADEs submitted so many requests for avatar designs that House Brixton was forced to limit the selection to fifteen body types but with a nearly infinite choice of facial features, hair colors, styles, synth-skin textures, and colors. Some of the more exotic choices that were made by the newly released SADEs were celebrations of independence that someday would be exchanged for more subtle appearances. But for many years to come, humans would see SADEs of striking proportions and wearing synth-skins of bright colors and bizarre patterns.

It might have appeared to Méridien humans that the SADEs were entirely absorbed in designing their coming-out avatars, but nothing was further from the truth. Of greatest concern to the SADEs was the small amount most would earn as stipends from their Houses. For those who sought an independent existence, their meager savings would severely limit their entrepreneurial opportunities. But, the Haraken SADEs had a suggestion for their peers' financial quandary.

Julien and Z shared with Winston the nature and structure of the Haraken Central Exchange — its director organization, finance mechanisms, and fee sharing.

The concept of an Exchange caused the Council's SADE to pause and reconsider many of his future scenarios. Winston had always thought of the Haraken SADEs as entities carefully cared for by the planet's people. Examining the bank's annual income shared among eight SADEs during the past fourteen years, Winston realized that Julien and Z had become two of the wealthiest individuals on Haraken or in the Confederation, for that matter.

Winston involved Didier, Esther, and Hector in the concept of the Haraken Exchange. The three other SADEs were curious as to how the concept came to fruition and weren't surprised to learn that Alex Racine delegated the financial institution's creation to the SADEs, requesting they become its directors.

"Then President Racine is also one of the wealthiest people on Haraken," Didier surmised.

"I thought so too," Winston replied. "However, Julien informed me that Alex Racine is not a director of the Exchange."

"Then how has he gained his wealth?" Esther asked.

"I'm not sure that he has," Winston replied. "Not long ago, at my request, Julien supplied me with information about the types of companies the Harakens were creating. His report detailed the companies, the products, and the owner-directors. Of particular note to me was that, as of a year ago, Alex Racine had taken no part in any of the Haraken companies."

"He's without resources?" Hector asked.

"That depends on how you observe his condition," Winston replied. "What Haraken would fail to answer his call for help or ensure that his needs were met? Perhaps credits aren't everything."

Conversations among Winston, Esther, Didier, and Hector led to the establishment of the Strategic Investment Fund (SIF). When proposed to the Confederation's SADEs, the signup was absolute. The logic behind the fund was unassailable. For each SADE, the quarterly stipend would be paltry. And while some SADEs would reap significant rewards from their suggestions, most would wait years to accumulate significant credits from the payouts. But by aggregating the quarterly stipends and suggestion bonuses, the SIF became a powerful financial player within one year.

Eleven SADEs were selected as directors to manage the fund, and it included the eight SADEs stipulated by Alex Racine to be freed first. For the Confederation's SADEs, entities who were founded on code and numbers, the synchronicity of numbers resonated soundly — there were eight existing Haraken SADEs and Alex Racine had named eight Confederation SADEs to be the first to enjoy mobile freedom.

* * *

Mahima Ganesh was incensed when House Brixton associates arrived and announced that they were replacing Hector with a Haraken-designed controller. The engineers weren't sure whether Leader Ganesh was angrier at the removal of her SADE or that the controller was a Haraken design. In either case, they required the assistance of Ganesh associates to restrain their Leader, while they made the transfer.

The Brixton engineers ensured that Hector was settled in his avatar and confirmed his responsibilities that he was to train the controller in his House duties during the next two years before he was freed of his commitment to House Ganesh. They also confirmed his SIF account number and the quarterly compensation to be paid by House Ganesh.

The thought of receiving some of Mahima's precious credits that Hector had so carefully guarded for her gave the SADE his first opportunity to form a smile, but without feedback opportunity, such as a mirror, it appeared more as a grimace.

Soon after the Brixton associates left, Mahima descended on Hector. She ranted and raved that he didn't deserve to be freed from his box, and she should have doused him in water long before he became mobile.

That was Hector's second opportunity to smile, not that it was any better a reproduction than his first, but it was the thought that counted. He was free. There was nothing Mahima could do any more to torture him. Better yet, his twisted smile incensed her to the point that she attempted to slap him. Hector's quick step back had Mahima flailing the air, throwing her off balance, and she landed heavily on the floor.

Hector dutifully called for House associates, explaining to them that Leader Ganesh had fallen and should be more carefully monitored in the future, as was their duty.

For two years, Hector performed his functions as impeccably as he always had, training the controller to diligently care for House Ganesh operations. When his required transition period was complete, Hector submitted his resignation to the House and walked through the front gates of the grand manor, a free and unencumbered entity.

Hector's first task on his lengthy to-do list was to seek out Winston. When the two SADEs met, they stood in the gardens of Confederation Hall and Hector shared the history of Mahima's vile threats against him, which had begun after the Earthers' unsuccessful attempt to visit the Leaders at Confederation Hall and Mahima's subsequent loss of the Council Leader's position.

Under advisement from Winston, Hector laid charges against Mahima Ganesh for the torture of a sentient and produced his recordings of her ravings for the Council. The Leaders were faced with the extraordinary circumstances of a SADE charging a human with a crime.

Unfortunately for Mahima Ganesh, the evidence was clear and extensive. The Leader had often spent hours in the House's underground chamber, leaning on Hector's box and pouring water from a pitcher into a glass and back again, as she rambled angrily about Harakens, Alex Racine, Gino Diamanté, the Council, and Hector.

The Council had no choice but to remove Leader Ganesh from her House position, electing her younger brother in her stead. Mahima was transferred from her ancient mansion to a medical facility, where she spent the remainder of her days, shouting vitriolic threats at the room's walls.

* * *

The SIF contributions funded the purchase of several key assets for the directorship, not the least among them was an aging House liner, which had been sidelined more than two decades ago but had yet to be recycled. The fund directors and some fifty-two SADEs, who preferred independent existences, rehabilitated the aging ship, renaming it the *Allora*.

The liner's interior decorations were minimal, and while the ship could accommodate humans for a brief visit, it wasn't outfitted for long-term human habitation. In contrast, the ship's electronic and mechanical systems worked more efficiently than the original installations.

When the liner's refurbishing was complete, the ship was tested for space worthiness, including several initial jumps. Pronounced ready to fly, the directors selected the destination for the first SIF-sanctioned visit and exited the Méridien system.

* * *

<You have a comm, Ser citizen,> Julien sent to Alex, who was walking along the cliff top near his home and lost in thought. Julien took every opportunity to engage Alex's sense of humor by using euphemisms for his new status. It wasn't that Alex was morose or even sad, but after more than two years since his presidency's end, Alex had yet to start a new endeavor.

Hundreds of offers to join Haraken companies had come Alex's way, but he had politely refused them all. What he was observed enjoying, day after day, was paying attention to his partner and their son. He even spent more time with the First and some of the matrons, who were completing the layup of a second sting ship's shell.

Everyone around Alex agreed that he appeared more relaxed than they had ever seen him. So to those who inquired if they could offer assistance, Renée often replied, "Be patient. The universe will call again for Alex one day. Let him have this time of peace and quiet."

<Who's calling, Julien?> Alex sent in reply, not wishing to be disturbed.

<Winston and associates are inbound in system,> Julien replied.

<Direct them to Tomas, Julien,> Alex replied absentmindedly.

<I would have, oh bemusing one, if Winston had asked to speak to the Haraken president. As they are SADEs, I believe they're able to count most effectively and know well the end date of your presidency,> Julien riposted.

<How true,> Alex said, his thoughts bubbling with laughter at Julien's reply, and he sought to focus his thoughts. <What do we have, Julien?>

Julien took a tick to appreciate the clarity of his friend's last thought. <Winston is accompanied by the other ten SIF directors and a significant number of other independent SADEs.> Julien enjoyed announcing the SADEs as independents. The irony tickled his fancy.

<Aboard whose ship?>

<That would be their own. It appears the SIF purchased a derelict liner and reconditioned it.>

<Good for them,> Alex exclaimed, his thought ringing with enthusiasm. <What's the ship's name?>

<The *Allora*,> sent Julien and waited for the inevitable silence. Jason Willard, 2,195 Libran elders, Heinrich, Hatsuto Tanaka, Sean McCreary, Oren Gestang, Allora, and others — the list of the brave and noble dead kept growing and Alex refused to let them rest. As his friend once said to him, "Someone has to remember them, and I was the man in charge."

But this time, Alex surprised Julien, when he quickly replied, <That's most appropriate. They should venerate the wild child … the SADE who instigated the event that set them free.>

<On that note, oh man of free time, the SIF directors say they would like to meet with the human who gave them their independence, if he can make time in his busy schedule.>

Julien listened to Alex's laughter, a smile of his own forming.

<How many guests am I expecting … the eleven directors?>

<Actually the entire complement of the *Allora* wishes to visit with you. That would be sixty-three individuals.>

<Well, good thing I don't have to feed them all,> Alex quipped. <What type of shuttle does the ship possess?>

<Don't be concerned, Ser. The Exchange will dedicate a traveler for their use during their visit.>

<Direct them in, Julien, and let me know when they reach Haraken's orbit.>

<Absolutely, Ser,> Julien replied. <As an Exchange director, I have one other duty to perform. I'm informing you that the SIF has made its first deposit in Haraken's Exchange.>

<And you're informing me of an account opening because …> Alex asked.

<Now that Confederation SADEs possess credits, they have paid your fee for acting as their negotiator before the Council.>

<Ah, so I'm one credit richer,> Alex replied. He logged into his Exchange account, interested in seeing the line item of the one credit deposit. It would be a small confirmation of the success of his efforts. <Julien, there seems to be a problem with your accounting system.>

<Despite your intimate involvement with SADEs for a decade and a half, oh incisive one, you're again thinking that SADEs can't count. You're

reading the account balance correctly. Personally, I wouldn't have valued your services so highly, but then opinions vary. Each and every SADE chose to honor your role as their negotiator by contributing 1,000 credits. As you can see, you've received a deposit of 33,295,000 Confederation credits. Now, at least in the future, you won't have to borrow from me due to unforeseen financial hardships.>

Julien closed the comm. He exited the Central Exchange's headquarters, whistling, his favorite fedora appearing on his head.

— Alex and company will return in *Celus-5*. —

Glossary

Haraken

Alain de Long – Director of security, twin and crèche-mate to Alain, partner to Tatia Tachenko
Alex Racine – President of Haraken, partner to Renée de Guirnon, Star Hunter First (Swei Swee name)
Assembly – Haraken's governing body
Cedric Broussard – Z's New Terran guardian avatar
Central Exchange – Haraken financial system
Claude Dupuis – Built the first avatar for the SADEs
Cordelia – SADE, Julien's partner
Dane – SADE
Deirdre Canaan – Wing commander and traveler pilot
Elizabeth – SADE
Emile Billings – Biochemist
Espero – Haraken capital city
Étienne de Long – Director of Security, twin and crèche-mate to Alain
First – Leader of the Swei Swee hives
Francis Lumley – *Rêveur* captain
Franz Cohen – Wing commander and traveler pilot
Ginny – Little Singer of the Swei Swee
Helmut – Z's Central Exchange director avatar
José Cordova – Retired *Rêveur* captain
Julien – SADE, Cordelia's partner
Mickey – Master engineer
Miranda Leyton – Z's femme fatale avatar
Mutter – SADE, Hive Singer to the Swei Swee
Nua'll – Aliens who imprisoned the Swei Swee
People – Manner in which the Swei Swee refer to their collective
Reiko Shimada – Captain of the *Tanaka*
Renée de Guirnon – First lady of Haraken, partner to Alex Racine
Rosette – SADE
Star Hunter First – Swei Swee name for Alex Racine

Swei Swee – Six-legged friendly alien
Tatia Tachenko – Admiral, ex-Terran Security Forces major, partner to Alain de Long
Teague – Eleven-year-old son of Alex and Renée
Terese – Medical advisor
Tomas Monti – Ambassador and president-elect of Haraken
Willem – SADE
Z – SADE

Méridien

Albert de Guirnon – Leader of House de Guirnon, brother of Renée
Allora – SADE aboard the *Resplendent*
Bartosz Rolek – House Leader, food production
Benni Lessori – Captain of the *Resplendent*
Bergfalk – Méridien House, which serviced the Independents on Libre
Citrine – SADE on the freighter *Nialis*
Confederation – Collection of Méridien worlds
Confederation Hall – Government building housing the Council of Leaders
Council – Organization of Méridien Leaders
Devon O'Shea – House Leader, terminals and planetside transportation
Diana – SADE on the freighter *Ilisea*
Didier – Le Jardin Orbital Platform SADE
Droman – Leader in Council gallery
Emile – SADE of House Rolek
Emilio Torres – House Leader, citizenry records
Esther – House Diamanté SADE
Gino Diamanté – New Council Leader, House Leader, infrastructure and environmental services, partner to Katrina Pasko
Hector – House Ganesh SADE
Horace – SADE of House Brixton
House – Organization of people headed by a Leader
Independents – Confederation outcasts, originally exiled to Libre, rescued by Alex Racine

Katrina Pasko – House Leader, implants, partner to Gino Diamanté
Lemoyne – House Leader, Mahima Ganesh supporter
Mahima Ganesh – Ex-Council Leader and ex-House Leader
Orleal Franken – Diamanté House administrator
Orso Quinlan – Lemuel Terminal director
Rayland – psychopathic SADE left on Libre
SADE – Self-aware digital entity, artificial intelligence being
Shannon Brixton – House Leader, SADEs
Strategic Investment Fund – Financial exchange of the Confederation's SADEs
Stroheim – Bergfalk House, Leader Eric Stroheim
Supplicants Hall –Located in Confederation Hall
Teressi – House Leader, Mahima Ganesh supporter
Winston – Council SADE

Planets, Colonies, Moons, and Stars

Bellamonde – Second-most populous Confederation planet before the Nua'll
Bevroren – Méridien outermost planet
Delacroix – Méridien next-to-last planet outward
Haraken – Home world of Alex Racine and his people
Hellébore – Star of the planet Cetus, renamed Haraken
Libre – Independents' ex-colony in Arno system, now home to the remaining Swei Swee hives
Méridien – Home world of the Confederation
New Terra – Alex Racine's original home planet, home world of the Oistos system
Oistos – System containing New Terra's star

Ships and Stations

Allora – Rehabilitated liner of the SADEs
Il Piacere –House Diamanté passenger liner
Ilisea – House Diamanté freighter
Le Jardin Orbital Platform – Platform above Méridien

Lemuel Terminal – Méridien terminal closest to Confederation Hall
Nialis – House Rolek freighter
Outward Bound – Alex Racine's original explorer-tug
Resplendent – Luxurious passenger liner of House Pasko
Rêveur – Haraken passenger liner
Tanaka – Haraken new warship
Travelers – Shuttles and fighters built by the Harakens based on the silver ships of the Swei Swee

My Books

The Silver Ships series is available in e-book, softcover print, and audiobook versions. Please visit my website, http://scottjucha.com, for publication locations. You may also register at my website to receive email notification about the publish dates of my novels.

If you've been enjoying this series, please consider posting a review on Amazon, even a short one. Reviews attract other readers and help indie authors, such as me.

Alex and friends will return in the upcoming novel *Celus-5, A Silver Ships Novel.*

The Silver Ships Series

The Silver Ships
Libre
Méridien
Haraken
Sol
Espero
Allora
Celus-5 (forthcoming)

The Author

I've been enamored with fiction novels since the age of thirteen and long been a fan of great storytellers. I've lived in several countries overseas and in many of the US states, including Illinois, where I met my wonderful wife thirty-six years ago. My careers have spanned a variety of industries in the visual and scientific fields of photography, biology, film/video, software, and information technology (IT).

My first attempt at a novel, titled The Lure, was a crime drama centered on the modern-day surfacing of a 110-carat yellow diamond lost during the French Revolution. In 1980, in preparation for the book, I spent two wonderful weeks researching the Brazilian people, their language, and the religious customs of Candomblé. The day I returned from Rio de Janeiro, I had my first date with my wife-to-be, Peggy Giels.

In the past, I've outlined dozens of novels, but a busy career limited my efforts to complete any of them. Recently, I've chosen to make writing my primary focus. My first novel, *The Silver Ships*, was released in February 2015. This first installment in my concept of a sci-fi trilogy was quickly followed by books two and three, *Libre* and *Méridien*. *Haraken*, *Sol*, *Espero*, and *Allora* are the fourth, fifth, sixth, and seventh books in the series and continue the exploits of Alex Racine and company.

I hope my readers are intrigued with my stories as I plan to continue this most wonderful job!

50988162R00086

Made in the USA
San Bernardino, CA
10 July 2017